A PLACE
WHERE MEMORIES
AND DREAMS
MEET

A PLACE WHERE MEMORIES AND DREAMS MEET

•

LYNDA STOWE LANDERS

AVALON BOOKS
THOMAS BOUREGY AND COMPANY, INC.
401 LAFAYETTE STREET
NEW YORK, NEW YORK 10003

PRINTED IN THE UNITED STATES OF AMERICA
ON ACID-FREE PAPER
BY HADDON CRAFTSMEN, SCRANTON, PENNSYLVANIA

This one is for my girls, Leigh and Brett

Chapter One

Driving past Grant's Barber Shop, Meredith Grant waved at her Uncle Bud. She knew he would be watching for her van, as would Uncle Joe and Aunt Fran at Grant's Market two doors down, her brother Andy from his service station on the corner, and her brother-in-law Travis at his drugstore across the street.

And dollars to doughnuts the phone was already ringing at the courthouse, to inform Sheriff Grant that his daughter had arrived safely from the "big city." As her mother always said, in Crystal Creek it was telegraph, telephone, or tell-a-Grant.

Meredith turned left off Main under the flashing amber signal light onto Fillmore Street. The voices of children pumping on swings and careening down slides in the park drifted in with the sounds of barking dogs and lawn sprinklers. Sun and clouds were playing an interesting game of hide-and-seek; at the moment the sun was winning. One block west, on Lincoln Street, was the house where Meredith had spent the first eighteen years of her life, and where her parents still lived.

But straight ahead, where Fillmore dead-ended into eight acres of greenbelts, trees, and rolling terrain, was the reason Meredith was here early on this Monday morning instead of in Dallas finishing the Swiss Avenue job.

"The House of the Seasons has been bought at auction and the new owner's already moved in," her dad had informed her over the telephone on Saturday. "And guess what, Mere, he's looking for a decorator!" The job was hers . . . if she wanted it. Was there ever any doubt?

And here she was, thirty miles from her present home, reliving cherished childhood memories.

The House of the Seasons was as much a part of her past as the Fourth of July fireworks in the park she'd just passed. Meredith couldn't count the times she and her brothers and sisters had played there when Aunt Fran was the full-time director of the staff at the mansion, although Meredith was the only one of the six Grant children who had fantasized about living there. Paul said old man Benjamine's ghost haunted the place, and because Paul was the oldest the others believed him. Except for Meredith, who'd always had a mind of her own and dreams to dream. Perhaps that was why she was the only Grant to leave Crystal Creek permanently—and the gap between here and Dallas was much more than thirty miles!

For many Texans who were keen on architecture or had a sense of the grotesque, the buildings in this Sam Houston County Courthouse town were the main event. With a population of 2,600, Crystal Creek had about a hundred buildings with Texas historic markers. A star in the parade of restored homes had once been the House of the Seasons, a huge, one-hundred-twenty-year-old structure whose present season looked like a losing one.

Turning into the weed-choked drive of the forlorn old house, Meredith slumped over the steering wheel and took in the three-story estate that looked like a birthday cake. She felt like bawling. How could this have happened to her beautiful house?

For years the place had drawn tens of thousands of visitors for guided tours. That had changed about the same time that Meredith went away to college. The daughter of the man who built the house—old man Benjamine—had died at the age of ninety-five, leaving everything to a niece who lived somewhere up north, and she had been covetous of the antiques, not the old house; after hauling off most of the contents she'd put the house up for sale. Unfortunately, nobody in Crystal Creek had the funds to purchase it, and neither did the town nor the county. So it had sat abandoned for almost seven years, until it became Sheriff Grant's duty to auction it off for back taxes.

Bright summer sun glinted off the cupola, where stained-glass windows suggested the seasons of the year—spring's green, summer's amber, fall's red, and winter's blue. Hence the name, the House of the Seasons. The mansion was a fine example of the transition period between Greek Revival and Victorian, with Italianate tall arched windows and bracketed cornices. But in its present state it didn't look fine at all; it seemed to be crumbling into its crabgrass lawn. Not merely unkempt, but unloved. That was what broke Meredith's heart.

The interior was sort of Romance Gothic; it was dim, musty, and a little dusty. Meredith's heels clicked over the scarred wooden floors. Her fingers probed gently along mildewed wallpaper. A circular opening in the first-floor ceiling displayed frescoes in the dome. She clambered up the stairs that wound up to the cupola, explored the dusty attic, then went down to rummage in the dank basement. After she had poked about to her heart's content, she returned to the library where she'd left her briefcase and settled back in a window seat. Floor-to-ceiling bay windows provided a glimpse of sky and foliage, the wooded backyard that dropped off to the creek from which the town took its name. She savored the view, then snapped open her briefcase and took out her notepad.

The House of the Seasons was unlike any place she had decorated. It had been built solidly, to last, anchored firmly to the top of the highest point in the county, and no amount of neglect could strip this wonderful house of its pretension to grandeur. All it needed was a gentle, loving nudge—and people. Meredith had always thought it was a little sad that there had not been any permanent residents to nurture this house for so many years, just strangers, tourists paying a couple of bucks to visit.

She gazed dreamily around the room, pen poised motionless over her notepad. For all its imposing grandiosity, the House of the Seasons had also seemed cozy and homey, to her, at least. And she knew she could bring back the grace, show the house that it could be beautiful again. Most of the mansion dated back to 1872, but parts were older, maybe antebellum, and she intended to painstakingly restore it to mint julep condition.

Pushing a ginger-colored curl back from her forehead, Meredith frowned. She didn't like the impersonal way she had been handed this job. The house had been bought by Cal Bonner, one of *the* Bonners, but a secretary from the Sunmedia corporate offices in Dallas had made all the arrangements with Meredith's dad. After inspecting the place Meredith found it difficult to believe that anyone even lived here. What little furniture there was looked suspiciously like it came from the rent-to-own place her cousin Billy opened last year over on

Washington Street, which was tantamount to turning Scarlett O'Hara into a bag lady!

"Well, I'll take care of that as soon as possible," Meredith declared to the empty room. A promise to herself, and the house she had dreamed of owning as far back as her memory went.

She shook her head ruefully, pulling herself away from the memories. She was no longer a wistful child but a twenty-five-year-old adult with her own interior decorating business. And she was very proud of that business, no matter how much she sometimes had to struggle to keep herself financially afloat. She hadn't thought about the House of the Seasons in a long while. She had just taken a bountiful trip back through time.

But she didn't have time to daydream now. She began jotting down page after page of notes, all her creativity brought to life as she planned new possibilities for the house. She had seen some lovely antique carpeting over in Midlothian last week. And for the dining room she wanted a rug that would mirror the decorative molding on the ceiling. The sink in the laundry room was badly cracked and had to be replaced. Meredith wrote faster as her visions for the house deepened in color and vividness; her fingers grew cramped from their intense, eager pressure on the pen.

The knocker pounded against the front door, interrupting Meredith's train of thought. She glanced at her watch and nodded in approval. The contractors she'd hired were on schedule. She slid away from the window seat and stretched her lower back exuberantly. She'd never been this excited over a decorating job. Humming under her breath, she went to let the workmen inside.

Soon the house echoed with intriguing sounds—nails screeching out of old boards, toolboxes clattering cheer-

6 *Lynda Stowe Landers*

fully. The house seemed to welcome the noise and confusion, creaking comfortably at its joints. Meredith was busy the rest of the morning and into the afternoon. She consulted with carpenters and electricians, stacked her carpet samples in the hall, and took down the musty draperies in the dining room. She desperately needed her assistant, but her sister, Kayanne, was in Dallas, finishing the Swiss Avenue house.

Hurrying through the downstairs hallway, Meredith stooped as she ran into a tangle of wires that spewed from the ceiling. She skirted a stepladder in the foyer and held up a swatch of wallpaper in the light of the landing windows. Ivy leaves or sprigs of violets? She'd better get some other samples before making that decision. The hall would convey the welcoming nature of the house.

"What the devil's going on here?" came a deep masculine voice behind Meredith, somehow making itself heard above the hammering and shouting. She swiveled and found herself looking into angry blue-green eyes. The gaze was intense and strangely compelling. Meredith fingered her wallpaper samples, unable to look away.

"Mr. Bonner?" she guessed. "Hi, I'm Meredith Grant—"

"I don't care if you're the Wizard of Oz. I want to know what a wrecking crew is doing in my house."

Meredith smiled indulgently—the smile she kept in reserve for difficult clients. "Perhaps we could talk where it's quieter," she suggested, leading the way into the library. She closed the beveled doors. "There, that's better."

Cal Bonner threw his jacket onto the ugly sofa and loosened his tie. "I just wanted some paint slapped on around the place. Nothing was said about demolition crews.''

"It's only minor repairs, Mr. Bonner. Necessary repairs, I might add, that shouldn't be covered by a 'little paint.' '' She allowed the slightest sarcasm to creep into her voice. "After all, the place has been vacant for over seven years, and—"

"That's not your decision to make." He raked a hand through blond hair that was already thoroughly rumpled. "Look, I've just spent the longest day of my life trying to bring what passes for a newspaper in this town into the twentieth century. All I want is a cold Pepsi and peace and quiet. Do you think you could do something about that?''

Meredith frowned at the autocratic tone of this son of privilege. She held back her first biting response. "You can forget the cold Pepsi, Mr. Bonner. There's something wrong with the wiring. I'm having it checked, but your fridge isn't working too well.'' She gave him an encouraging look, only to have him glare balefully back at her.

"You're an interior decorator, right?" he rasped out.

"Yes, of course—"

"So you're not an electrician, and you shouldn't be messing with my wiring.''

"I'm not. I called in a very qualified man to do the job. I can personally vouch for him—''

"There's nothing in our contract about electricians,'' he said ominously. "And nothing about people tearing down my walls. Do I need to remind you, Ms. Grant, that our agreement is a binding legal document?''

Meredith folded her arms. "I'm aware of that, Mr. Bonner. My brother is an attorney, right here in Crystal Creek. But I should never had signed that agreement without meeting you. That is something I never do. Good interior design can be accomplished only after several consultations, and—''

''Ms. Grant, don't lecture me. Just do something about that racket!''

Meredith clenched her teeth. No way could she muster up her difficult-client smile again. She did manage a stiff nod before retreating from the room. Once on the other side she allowed herself a full grimace. Of all the people in the world, why did it have to be this jerk who bought the House of the Seasons? It just wasn't fair. Cal Bonner didn't deserve this place.

''The client is always right,'' she muttered with absolutely no conviction, as she made the rounds to call off her forces.

After everyone had finally trooped out, she returned to the library, intending to be pleasantly persuasive, if it killed her. Instead, she found Cal Bonner fast asleep, his head cushioned against the back of that hideous sofa, his feet propped up on the coffee table.

Meredith all at once lost her steam. The man no longer looked combative—just tired. She tiptoed to the window seat to retrieve her briefcase. She paused at the door on her way out, her eyes lingering on the man. Even asleep there was a vibrancy about him, a blond attractiveness that drew her much too naturally.

She shook herself. It didn't seem right to stand here looking at him like this. His tall, broad-shouldered body was as defenseless as a baby at the moment, especially with those whimsical argyle socks adorning his feet. Unable to control a smile, Meredith slipped out the front door.

She was back bright and early the next morning, and as she angled her van up the driveway and around to the back of the house, her old exuberance returned. Mr. Bonner's red Jaguar was still parked next to the small building that was occupied during Prohibition by a bootlegger. So much for sneaking her troops in this morning. She swung out of the van and stood back to observe the house from a rear view. Sun bounced off the four stained-glass windows in the cupola, creating a rainbow of dazzling colors on the flagstone path. Instead of contributing a cheery air, however, it only seemed to emphasize the melancholy mood of graying wood that was peeling off the second-floor balcony. Untended shrubbery almost completely hid the seven dormers that had an eastern exposure, and the twin chimneys poked up above it all like a couple of partygoers who didn't know when to go home. The entire house seemed to be shrinking from the outside in. Meredith moved a step closer. She'd give the house back its confidence and pride no matter how many roadblocks Mr. Cal Bonner put up.

Nodding in satisfaction, armed with her briefcase, she marched up the flagstone walkway to the back porch.

There was no answer after several knocks. Meredith rummaged in her briefcase and took out the key her dad had given her. "Hello?" She poked her head inside the door. Again there was no response. She crossed through the screened-in porch, into the laundry room and kitchen, and headed for the window seat in the library. She glanced disapprovingly at the Pepsi can and dried crust of bread on the coffee table. Humming to herself, she pulled out her notepad and began jotting down reminders. She wanted the carpenters to build cherrywood cabinets in the kitchen, a bookshelf in the cupola. And the dry sink she'd special-ordered would be delivered this week; perhaps it would look best in one of the guest bedrooms.

"Do you always wander into people's houses uninvited, Ms. Grant?"

Meredith turned and found herself blushing uncomfortably. Cal Bonner was standing in the doorway, dripping wet, with nothing but a towel wrapped around his waist. She averted her eyes quickly from the tangled mat of damp hair on his broad chest. But the strong, powerful lines of his body were already etched into her mind. She swallowed. With difficulty.

"Um . . . good morning, Mr. Bonner."

"I told you not to come back," he said brusquely. "What part of the message didn't you understand?"

"No, you didn't, actually. We didn't get that far yesterday. And don't pay any attention to me. I'll get to work while you . . . um . . . go on with whatever."

"You're not supposed to be doing any work."

"Mr. Bonner, about our discussion yesterday—"

"There wasn't a discussion. You're going to cease ripping my house apart. Period." As he spoke, his eyes traveled over Meredith with frowning thoroughness. He examined her ginger-colored curls that cascaded down her back and tended to frizz in the summer humidity, her green eyes, the faint but stubborn smatter of freckles across her nose. It was impossible to tell from his expression whether or not she had passed inspection. *What difference did it make, for crying out loud?* This wasn't a beauty contest, it was a job! She concentrated on searching through her briefcase.

"Why don't we sit down with a cup of tea and talk this over?" she said in a reasonable tone. "Mint's the best . . . here's some."

He glanced skeptically from her briefcase to the tea bags she was holding up, then back to her briefcase. A smile tugged at the corners of his mouth.

"No, thanks," he said dryly. "I'll stick to coffee. Strong and black."

He turned back into the hallway. Meredith hurried after him. He pulled up so abruptly that she almost bumped against him. She breathed a heady whiff of clean skin and fresh soap before she backed away. She was wearing heels, but in bare feet he still towered over her.

"Look what you've done," he muttered, gesturing at clumps of wires and chunks of plasterboard.

"Minor repairs. I told you—"

"They don't look minor to me." He peered at the walls, as if expecting them to come tumbling down around him. "Good-bye, Ms. Grant. Don't let the door hit you on your way out. You can settle up your account with . . . whatever that dingbat's name is over at the newspaper who handles such things."

Meredith glared at him. "That dingbat happens to be my cousin . . . and her name is Ellen."

"It figures," he said with soft sarcasam. "Don't let me keep you, Ms. Grant, and just be grateful that I'm not suing for damages."

Feeling stunned, Meredith stood very still. She had never been fired from a job before. This couldn't be happening. She wouldn't allow it to happen!

She was beside him when he reached the upstairs landing. "Mr. Bonner, we have an agreement. You said yourself that it's a binding document."

"Only if both parties abide by the terms. You've gone way too far."

"Mr. Bonner—"

"I'm going to finish my shower now. Do you intend to follow me in there, too?"

"Of course not," she said stiffly, watching his muscular calves until they disappeared around the corner.

Good legs shouldn't be wasted on such a grouch. He was worse than impossible. Meredith sank down on the first step, drawing up her knees. Cal Bonner made her feel as if all her years of hard work were on the line here. It had been a struggle to make Grant Designs a success. She couldn't afford to lose this job—and not just for financial reasons. The House of the Seasons needed her. That was all there was to it.

When he came downstairs again, fully clothed this time in a pair of khaki slacks and a red polo shirt, Meredith was in the kitchen with her tea bags. She had found two mugs and a jar of instant coffee in the bare cupboards. Cal gazed at her sardonically. He looked vibrant with energy, strong jaw freshly shaven and his thick blond hair only slightly repressed by dampness from the shower.

"You must like good-byes, Ms. Grant," he said. She watched in consternation as he twisted the lid from a jar of peanut butter, and then opened a box of Ding Dongs.

"Is that what you're having for breakfast?" she asked.

"As a matter of fact it is. Why?"

"Yogurt would be healthier."

He ripped the cellophane off one of the Ding Dongs, dipped it in the peanut butter, and took a bite. "When I want your advice, Ms. Grant, I'll ask for it. Good-bye." With the Ding Dong clamped firmly between his white teeth, he reached for a battered pan and started filling it with water.

Meredith grabbed the pan from him and finished filling it at the leaky faucet. "I know we can clear up this misunderstanding," she told him firmly. "The thing of it is, I assumed I was to use my own judgment, since I heard nothing to the contrary. My dad said—" She paused for accusatory emphasis. "My dad said you weren't interested in discussing details."

"I don't even know your father."

"Sure you do. He's—"

"The sheriff," he finished for her, understanding suddenly dawning in his eyes. "Sheriff Grant. Of course. I should have made the connection. Ellen Grant, my assistant at the *Chronicle*. And I believe there's also a Grant who's an attorney?"

"Paul," she supplied. "His office is on Polk Street. Directly behind—"

"Grant's Barber Shop."

She shook her head. "Grant's Texaco. My brother Andy owns that."

"Is there anybody in this town you're not kin to?"

Meredith shrugged. "What can I tell you? The Grants are a prolific bunch. Does that bother you?"

He struck a match and lit one of the stove burners. He took the pan back from Meredith. "What bothers me is what you're doing to my house. I think tearing down walls constitutes more than a detail."

"Maybe it does. But you don't even care about the House of the Seasons."

"It's a house. What do you expect me to do? Fall in love with it?"

"Well, yes."

"Then you're barking up the wrong tree. It's a place to stay for however long I have to be here. That's all. And if you want the truth, I don't even like it. Now, good-bye, again." He chomped down on the Ding Dong. Meredith sat on one of the narrow kitchen chairs and stared at him.

"There's some bread that's not too stale," she remarked. "I found it when I was looking for the mugs. Toasted in the oven, it might even be edible."

Cal straddled the chair across from her. "And I suppose you have jam in that briefcase of yours."

Meredith nodded. "Strawberry, grape, and maybe some apple. The unsweetened variety. Which one would you like?"

"Plying me with food isn't going to work, Ms. Grant."

"I'll keep the repairs to a minimum. And before you say anything, please hear me out. It's important to finish what I've started with the wiring. For safety's sake. Beyond that, there's just one section of the roof that can't be neglected, and—"

"Ms. Grant—"

"A bit of carpentry and one room to be replastered. That's all. And here's the good part. I'll make sure— absolutely sure—that everyone is gone whenever you're here. All you have to do is let me know when to clear out. Fair enough?"

The water was boiling. Cal dumped an alarming amount of coffee into his mug, swirling hot water on top of it. He glanced at Meredith's mug, hesitated, and then with a beleagured sigh poured some over her tea bag.

"You're a pack mule of a woman, Ms. Grant, and I admire your tenacity. But the answer is still no."

Meredith shook her head emphatically. "I was hired to do a job. Why have you suddenly changed your mind?"

"Because I suddenly had my house falling down around my ears."

Meredith's eyes blazed against the flint of his. "Mr. Bonner, give me one reason why you wouldn't want essential repairs to be made?"

He scowled at her for a long moment without saying anything. No one had ever regarded her with such patent disgust before. She lifted her chin almost defiantly. Cal Bonner definitely was not good for the ego.

"I'm sure it's a nice house," he muttered at last. "But I'm only here temporarily. I'll probably just have to sell it again."

"What do you mean?"

"It's a long story, and quite frankly it's none of your business. Look, I know you mean well, Ms. Grant, and, believe me, I do appreciate the historical significance of this house. But at the moment I've got my hands full trying to turn the *Chronicle* into a profitable business, and I don't need all this aggravation."

"You won't have any. I promise," she said earnestly. "You'll never know I'm here."

He drank his coffee, still frowning at her over the rim of his mug. Then he plunked the mug down on the table. "Show me what you intend to do," he said so suddenly that Meredith started and sloshed tea out of her mug. She recovered quickly and led him to the morning room, which was badly in need of work. Then she took him to the attic, where she discoursed on the value of minor patching now to avoid major flooding later.

"Enough!" Cal protested. "All right . . . I accept the roof job and the wiring, and maybe the other repairs— if I know I can count on coming home at night and not finding a wall or two missing."

"You have my word," Meredith said fervently, as her nose began to itch from all the dust in the attic. She tried to fish casually in her pockets for a tissue, only to have a handkerchief thrust at her just in time for her sneeze.

"Thank you." She peered over the handkerchief, glancing surreptitiously at Cal's feet; they were hidden in expensive loafers and it was impossible to tell if he was wearing fanciful argyle socks again today.

Her gaze traveled upward again to lock with those startling eyes. The attic suddenly seemed too intimate a place to be conducting a business transaction. Perhaps it was the lowness of the ceiling, or the presence of rotting boxes and chests that bespoke old memories. She folded the handkerchief and tried cramming it into one of her strictly decorative pockets.

''I'll return this to you.'' She advanced cautiously toward the trapdoor. ''What is all this up here?'' she asked, brushing a film of dirt from the top of one of the boxes.

''I have no idea. This is the first time I've been up here. You're the expert on the place, aren't you?''

''I suppose they could belong to the Benjamines. Miss Ima was the last of them. She moved to a retirement home over in Dallas several years before her death. That's when the house was open to the public, at her request. To pay taxes and other expenses. After she passed away her niece claimed all the furnishings that were worth anything. She probably didn't find anything up here that she considered worth the effort.''

''And left them to be tossed out by the next owner,'' Cal said.

''Don't you dare! Haven't you ever heard the saying, one person's junk is someone else's treasure?''

''No,'' came his dry response as he disappeared down through the trapdoor. Meredith didn't relish the idea of advancing rear-view-first down the ladder, and turned around to face him again as soon as possible.

''Now, just tell me when you want me out of here today,'' she said in her most agreeable tone.

''You're in luck. I'll be working late at the newspaper.

I have the joyous task of converting dinosaurs over to computers today.''

''Wonderful! I mean, I'll stick to my end of the agreement. And you won't regret this, Mr. Bonner. You really won't.''

He gave her a look that said he was already regretting it. Downstairs again, he picked up his briefcase. ''So long, Ms. Grant.''

''You might as well call me Meredith,'' she said pertly.

He gave the idea a frown, but after a moment shrugged. ''Whatever. So long, Meredith.''

There was no reason her pulse should have quickened when he said her name. He'd pushed it out of his mouth grudgingly, in fact.

She was relieved when a moment later the Jaguar rolled down the drive. She scrambled to the phone and called the work force back to duty. Then she settled in the window seat to wait for them and savor her victory.

She allowed herself the luxury of slipping off her shoes and tucking her legs up. This window seat had been her favorite spot in the house as a child. Her own special place. Something pretty hard to find in the Grant household, which was bursting at its seams with children.

She smiled, remembering the House of the Seasons through a child's eyes. Her life had certainly changed. She'd worked her way through art school, studying and sketching for her classes late at night and on weekends. She hadn't enjoyed much of a social life, but she'd graduated with honors. Nothing could daunt her after that, not even the job selling floor tile. She simply made herself an expert on tiles and then moved on. Now, at twenty-five, she had her own business. She could be proud of her accomplishments, despite the skepticism of Cal Bonner.

She wasn't looking forward to working with him at all! Yet he was a puzzle to her. It was common knowledge that the Bonner-owned Sunmedia had recently purchased Suburban Publishers, which added several weeklies to a large group of radio and television stations and newspapers throughout the Southwest and Midwest. But nobody, in their wildest imagination, had expected one of *the* Bonners to personally run the *Chronicle,* much less relocate to Crystal Creek. And Cal Bonner was obviously as out of place in a small town as a bucket under a bull.

But he was only here temporarily, he'd said.

Well, as he'd indicated, it was none of her business why he was here or for how long.

Meredith fingered the corner of the handkerchief trailing out of her pocket. After a moment's hesitation she brought it up to her face and inhaled tentatively.

The handkerchief smelled of pine after-shave. Clean, brisk, masculine. She took a deep breath.

She opened her eyes wide. What was she doing? She stuffed the handkerchief unceremoniously back into her pocket. Swinging her legs down, she slipped her feet into her pumps where they belonged. She was determined about one thing. Cal Bonner or no Cal Bonner, the House of the Seasons was going to be the best work of her career.

Chapter Two

"Where have you two been?" Meredith demanded when her sister Kayanne finally arrived on the job, their teenaged brother, Bo, in tow. "You were supposed to be here twenty minutes ago—" She started, hearing the shrill octave of her voice. "Good grief, would you listen to me? I sound like Mother!"

"Mother hen would be more like it," her six-foot, four-inch "baby" brother said, biting back a grin.

And after a second Kayanne started to giggle, and two seconds later Bo started, and five seconds after that all three of them were laughing until tears ran down their faces. The mother hen and her two chicks, as they'd been known around town.

Childhood sweethearts Sam and Roxanne Grant were married ten months when their first child was born. That was Paul. Andy, Joleen, and Meredith had registered in before their parents could take a deep breath. By the time late arrivals Kayanne and Bo came along, Roxanne Grant was in a perpetual state of exhaustion, and "ask your sister Meredith, she'll know," became the rule of thumb. As if there were no one else in the house who could tell whether or not Kayanne should wear her sweater, or where Bo's basketball was. "Ask your sister Meredith." If she heard it once, she'd heard it a dozen times a day. She was the one who made sure Kayanne got to her Girl

Scout meetings and Bo to basketball practice. Rarely was she seen without the two youngest Grants trailing close behind. "Mother Meredith hen and her two baby chicks." And although Meredith never resented having that responsibility heaped on her young shoulders, it was a relief to go off to college, leaving Tommy Gene Beckett to marry Sue Ann Jefferson; together they were raising four little Becketts.

Meredith and Tommy Gene had gone steady all through high school. But her dreams had not included Tommy Gene, or having his or anybody else's children. She hadn't ruled out the possibility of falling in love, in the vagueness of "someday." However, she'd served her time, for the time being, and in the meantime she had bigger fish to fry—and she was still responsible for Kayanne and Bo and running interference!

"Bo wasn't home when I stopped by to pick him up, Mere," Kayanne explained, covering herself.

"Big deal," Bo said. "So I was five minutes late. I was shooting baskets over at the school with the guys."

"When weren't you shooting baskets with the guys?" Kayanne shot back. "You're paid to work, not to play stupid games. Tell him, Mere."

"You're paid to work, not play stupid games," Meredith repeated in a singsong voice. "Now, do you suppose we could get some of that work done?"

Both nodded their heads at the same time, then busied themselves with paintbrushes and rollers in the library. Meredith watched for a moment, admiring the smooth, meticulous strokes of Kayanne's brush. As usual, she was tedious about her work. Bo was slapdash in comparison. But, sibling eruptions aside, they were part of what made Grant Designs so special. "The Personal and Individual Touch"—that was how Meredith advertised, and she stuck by that motto. She herself always looked forward to completing the details of a job. She was an expert at wallpapering difficult corners and varnishing intricate moldings, and she knew how to put antiques or good reproductions together with necessary modern appointments.

Being so self-sufficient was an advantage, allowing her to make competitive bids against the larger decorating firms in the metroplex that hired out all their physical labor.

But business and financial motives played no part in her eagerness to work on the House of the Seasons . . . Cal Bonner's house, she grudgingly conceded. This place reached her emotions in a much deeper way. She was going to patch and mend many of its injuries herself, because no one else cared about it the way she cared. And the house called out to her with many needs.

Meredith left the carpenters and roofers under Kay-anne's supervision and took off for the shops in Farmer's Branch. She poked about happily for hours, looking for the right things to grace the House of the Seasons's empty rooms. She found a nineteenth-century genre painting for the upstairs hallway, along with gilt-framed horses for one wall of the dining room. And she doubted that Cal had a wok so she bought him one of those, too.

Her van began to overflow with bundles. She managed to squeeze in a Victorian chaise and a curly-maple rocker, but finally ran out of space. Twilight was drifting down by the time she returned to Crystal Creek. The house was deserted, all the workers gone, including Kay-anne and Bo. Meredith savored the solitude, her own special time to be creative. She was her own boss and didn't have to follow someone else's rigid schedule.

The house surrounded her with a lonely yet comfortable gloom as she arranged her purchases. A deep sense of contentment grew inside her, a feeling that was the house's unique gift to her. She pushed stray wisps of hair away from her face and phoned out for pizza. Then she gravitated to the morning room, carrying the hand-painted box on a stand she'd found in one of her favorite shops. The stand had a shelf for displaying plants or knickknacks. The wood box, with a floral design, had solid brass hardware. She'd known it would look perfect in the morning room. It was her best find of the day.

She glanced out the window just in time to see a shooting star scratching its fire across the sky. She didn't have time to wish on it. She took a plastic scraper and began the pleasurable task of chipping some hardened dirt away from the window frame. The perfect shade of paint for this room would be seafoam green, and she'd use plantation shutters instead of curtains. She could picture how the sun would look slanting through them at a perfect angle.

The front door creaked open forcefully, then banged shut again. Footfalls strode down the hall, and they did not sound happy. A moment later Cal's tall body filled the doorway. Meredith stared at him, scraper poised in her hand.

"What are you doing here?" she wailed.

"I live here, remember? And you swore to me, Ms. Grant—"

"Meredith."

"You swore I'd have peace and quiet tonight, did you not?"

"I did, and everybody else is gone. But you said you'd be working late."

"It *is* late."

She squinted at her watch. "It's not that late," she murmured hopefully.

"Exactly what is your defination of late?" He pried a sticky newspaper away from his foot.

"I don't know . . . later than this. Much later. Then it would really be late."

He let his irritation show, and Meredith moved hastily away from the window. "This won't happen again," she declared, then promptly tripped over a bucket of rags and landed in Cal's arms.

She caught her breath as she swayed against him. His face was very close to hers, eyes tantalizing under his definite brows. The dark shadow of a day's growth of beard emphasized his clean, healthy skin. With the top two buttons of his polo shirt undone, she could see a hint of his curling chest hair. She drew away, her breath coming unevenly.

"It's nice to be so graceful and well coordinated," Cal said with a glint of humor.

"How do you think I got crowned Princess Klutz of Crystal Creek High?" She tried a smile that didn't seem to fit. She felt his gaze. Then he took hold of her hand and examined its shape, stroking the inside of her wrist very lightly, very gently, with a slight frown, as if he didn't quite understand why he was doing this. Meredith's pulse throbbed. She snatched her hand away—or maybe he dropped it abruptly; it was hard to tell.

"I'll be out of here in thirty seconds," she said. "Everything is coming along wonderfully, by the way. This is a good, solid house . . . but you don't really care about construction, do you?"

"Not in the least, and now that we've established that, do you think we could get on with life?"

"Sure. I'm out of here." She popped into the library

and picked up her briefcase. Cal followed, leaning in the doorway to watch her. She was uncomfortably aware of her rumpled skirt and dusty blouse, but Cal's gaze swept away from her to the sheet-draped sofa.

"What are you doing in here?" he asked, yanking the sheet away.

"Painting. Isn't the color wonderful?" She gestured to a wall that was almost finished. "And we of course covered the furniture, even though it is atrocious. I think you'll be pleased with the new things I have in mind."

"Ms. Grant!"

"It's Meredith, or I suppose I could keep calling you Mr. Bonner, if you prefer—"

"I don't care what you call me. Just don't touch this couch."

"You're not serious. That sofa is horrible. It's outrageous. It'll spoil the whole room. Look at it, for crying out loud!"

"I like it. It's comfortable, and it's just the right length."

"If that's all that's bothering you, I can get you an extra-long sofa. Made to order, even." She automatically fell into her professional voice, the slightly dry observational tone that she used when dealing with clients on a sensitive point. A tone that seemed educated and patient at the same time, and often sold her viewpoint on its own.

Not this time.

"I don't want another couch," Cal said. "I want this one. That's it."

Meredith sighed explosively. "We can discuss it later."

"We *have* discussed it. Case closed."

"Okay," she grumbled, viewing the sofa with its

gaudy rose flowers set against a background of industrial gray. She doubted Goodwill would take it.

"Why don't I believe you?" he asked slowly.

She pretended to be offended. "My word is my bond, Mr. Bonner. It's your sofa, your house, and the customer is always right."

Cal glanced at her quizzically. Just then the knocker rapped at the front door. "Now who can that be?" he asked, rubbing his neck. "There's enough going on here already."

"Uh . . . well, Cal," Meredith said hestitantly. "You see, I didn't expect you back yet, and—" The knocker banged again. "I ordered pizza," she finished in a rush. She set her briefcase down and slipped past Cal to the front door. She returned bearing a large box.

"Mushrooms, green peppers, no cheese," she announced. "On a whole-wheat crust. It's yours, as an apology for me not keeping my end of the bargain. After today you won't know I exist."

He glanced around to the half-painted walls and the colorful sheets strewn about. "You don't strike me as a woman who fades into the woodwork," he said.

"I promise to disappear. Right now." She prodded the box into his hands. "Good-bye."

"Meredith . . ." He sighed. "Put two plates on the table, will you? I'll scare up something to drink."

She led the way into the kitchen, holding the swinging door open for him as Cal came through with the box.

"Thank you," he said dryly.

"You're welcome." She washed her hands and took a long, enjoyable time patting them dry on one of the linen towels she'd bought today. Then she hunted through the cupboards, but found only a few plastic plates. She made a mental note to do something about that first thing tomorrow. Cal brought out a lukewarm Pepsi from the refrigerator that still wasn't working properly. "We'll have to share," he said. "I haven't had time to go to the grocery store. I'm assuming there *is* one in this one-horse town."

Meredith nodded. "Grant's Market. On Main Street."

"Grant's Market? Now why doesn't that surprise me?" He located two jelly glasses. Meredith sat across from him, feet hooked around her chair legs, and tore off a piece of pizza.

"It's good," she said encouragingly. "Don't you think so?"

He raised the lid of the box. "Pizza Heaven? Is that for real?"

"Sure. They make the best pizza in town. Actually, it's the only place in Crystal Creek you can buy pizza, but it *is* good. Very nourishing, too."

"I suppose Pizza Heaven is another Grant-owned business."

"Wrong. It's owned by an old high school sweetheart of mine, Tommy Gene Beckett."

"Is he a health nut?"

"Hardly. Why?"

"Whole-wheat crust," he said disparagingly. "And how can a pizza possibly be any good without cheese and lots of meat?" But a moment later he added, "Not too bad."

Meredith sat back in triumph. Now and then Cal Bonner was almost human. If only she could convince him to get rid of that horrible sofa.

Bide your time, she told herself. Patience was a decorator's watchword. She'd dealt with many clients who hung on unreasonably to favorite pieces of furniture, and always, without exception, she was able to wean them, eventually. She could do the same with Cal Bonner, when the time was right.

She smiled confidently across at him and felt a quiver chase down her spine when he actually smiled back. She gulped some Pepsi, and started coughing. "It went down the wrong way," she gasped.

"Should I slap you on the back?"

"Don't you dare." She finally caught her breath. "You sound like you'd enjoy it too much."

"This pizza is really pretty good," he said, grinning noncommittally, as if the thought had occured to him.

"Good and healthy," Meredith said. "You really ought to think about improving your diet. All you have in the fridge is stale bread—white bread—and some very suspect mayonnaise. Actually, you don't have the mayonnaise anymore. I did you a favor and threw it out."

Cal's slice of pizza froze in the air midway to his mouth. "The inside of my refrigerator doesn't need decorating."

"You're right. It has to go. I have an idea for a new model. I saw one today that would be perfect. It's brand new, but looks old, if that makes any sense."

Cal chomped down viciously on his pizza. "The fridge stays."

"Maybe you're right. With a little refurbishing it could be very decorative. I could convert it to a storage area. Maybe have a couple of trailing plants on top of it. I'm partial to Boston ferns."

"I loathe Boston ferns. I hate plants. I want the fridge plugged into the wall, and I'll stock it with anything I please . . . including real mayonnaise."

Meredith set down her pizza and struggled to maintain a reasonable tone. "I always try to accommodate my clients' wishes, of course. I just didn't know you had any specific ideas for the house. Why don't you tell me how you envision the overall scheme?''

"I don't. I just wanted a little paint slapped up, and I was thinking more in terms of white."

"White paint?" she said disbelievingly.

"What else?"

"*Anything* else. Robin's-egg blue, for instance. Almond. Mauve—"

"Red. You're painting my library red!"

They glared at each other across the table.

"That happens to be sunset crimson," Meredith informed him stiffly.

"It still makes the room look as if it belongs in a brothel. Where did you buy something like that?"

"I mixed it myself."

His gaze seemed to soften. "It's fine."

"If you don't like it, just say so."

"I didn't mean to hurt your feelings."

"Don't be ridiculous. I'm a professional."

"Professionals can be just as susceptible to wounded feelings as anybody else."

"I'll paint over it. How about institutional white?" Meredith chewed her pizza vigorously.

"I knew it. Your feelings are hurt. Just leave it red dawn . . . or whatever."

"Mr. Bonner—"

"Cal."

"Let me explain to you one more time that feelings have absolutely nothing to do with this."

"I disagree. You're taking everything personally. Why not admit it? Then we can get on with the job."

Meredith took a deep breath. "All you have to do is tell me what you want done with your house. I'll be more than happy to comply."

"If I knew what I wanted, you wouldn't be here in the first place."

"White paint's it, then? That's your only opinion? I should have saved the mayonnaise. I could have slapped that on a few walls."

They ate the rest of the pizza in stubborn silence. Afterward Meredth stuffed the empty box into the trash and filled the sink with water.

"You need a drain board," she said. Cal didn't answer. The silence between them vibrated with a sultry tension as they stood side by side at the sink. Meredith's hands moved over the dishes in the sudsy water. Cal took the dishes from her, rinsed them, and dried them with a paper towel. Her heart was pulsing in her throat at his nearness.

His hand slid into the warm, soapy water. His fingers bumped gently against hers and he turned toward her. She parted her lips to protest, but no words would come out. She couldn't make herself step away from him. There was a sweet, heavy expectancy in her limbs.

His lips moved over her temple, brushing the line where her hair grew from a widow's peak. "Lovely," he murmured, his voice husky. "You are lovely, Meredith Grant." He brought her close to him—slowly, inexorably. His mouth descended to cover hers.

It was not a demanding kiss. It wasn't hurried. Cal made a leisurely exploration, discovering each subtle contour of her lips. His touch was like warm, golden honey spreading through her. It tantalized her, teasing with its gentleness. Her fingers reached out to twine with his in the water.

Meredith was suddenly frightened, the warmth inside her fanning into a flame. What was she doing?

"No!" The word came out as a strangled cry. She

struggled away from him, cradling her wet hands against her body.

"Meredith," he began, but she backed away from him. She didn't want to talk about it. It was bad enough that she had allowed it to happen.

She sucked in a deep breath, and then quickly said, "I'm going." She exhaled again. She ran to the hall, grabbed her briefcase, and fled out the door.

Her cheeks burned with confusion as her hands fumbled with her car keys, and she nearly flooded the van's engine when she started it up. Nothing seemed familiar to her anymore. She was relieved to make it out of the driveway.

She drove through town, connected with Highway 20, and, pushing the van as fast as she dared drive, headed for the northwestern tip of the Dallas area. Farmer's Branch was nestled amid the LBJ Freeway, Dallas North Tollway and Interstate 35.

Meredith and the bank owned one of the pre-World War II houses that had been converted to commercial usage in the eighties. She turned down the tree-lined street, glad to be here, for her heart was still beating a wild tattoo. She managed to park at the curb, then hurried up the stone walk to her front door. She didn't switch on any lights when she let herself in; she knew her way by memory. The downstairs she had converted into an office; the decor was French provincial. She followed the landing light she always left on when she was out at night up the stairs, and she was immensely relieved to reach her living quarters. She needed a safe harbor to calm herself and straighten out her emotions.

She extracted a tea bag from her briefcase and heated some water in the kitchen. A few moments later she was able to sink gratefully into her antique rocking chair. She rocked fiercely and sipped the tea.

Okay. So she was physically attracted to Cal Bonner. *Very* attracted to Cal Bonner, she silently ammended. What normal woman wouldn't be? And he had kissed her, tenderly and completely.

She launched herself from the rocker so swiftly it nearly tipped over backward, and took a turn around the carpet, nibbling at a thumbnail, her brain befuddled. She had to decide how she was going to handle this. She'd never been kissed by a client before. *No one* had kissed her like that, ever.

Admittedly, her experience was limited with this sort of thing. She'd always been too busy with her career to develop a serious relationship with a man. And now she had her own business, her own life. She was independent and happy. She wanted to keep things exactly that way. She certainly wasn't going to pursue what had happened tonight. She didn't need a man intruding on her hard-won independence. Especially not a man as dangerously attractive as Cal Bonner. A man like that could change a woman's life forever.

She wouldn't give him the opportunity. She'd keep her promise to stay well out of his path. She'd finish her work on the house and never see him again.

She sank back down into the rocker and picked up her cup. But mint tea wasn't comforting her tonight. She'd always been able to count on mint tea.

Now it was just growing cold in the cup. That was not a good sign.

Chapter Three

It seemed as though she had barely closed her eyes when Meredith was awakened by the persistent jangling of the telephone on her bedside table. She burrowed deeper under her pillow. She had tossed restlessly most of the night, dreaming she was in Cal Bonner's arms. She wasn't ready to face the world yet, but the telephone wouldn't stop ringing. She was forced to emerge from her cocoon.

"Hello?" she croaked into the receiver, rubbing her eyes against the early-morning sunlight. 8:15, she saw, bringing the clock close to her face.

"Hi, Mere. It's Ellen," came the disgustingly cheerful voice of her cousin. "I know you're cranky early in the morning, so I'll do all the talking. Mr. Bonner wanted me to call and arrange a meeting with you for this afternoon, four-thirty, at the Diamond Club. You lucky duck. I hear that's a really neat place, and Cal Bonner's not only drop-dead gorgeous, he's up to his navel in greenbacks. Four-thirty, Mere. Don't forget. See ya."

"Wait a minute," Meredith sputtered, struggling away from a tangle of sheet and blanket. The room was bathed in the cold air-conditioning air. "Ellen, what's this all about?"

"Beats me. I'm just the messenger. I'm still trying to figure out how to work these stupid computers he had installed. Somebody's on the other line, Mere. Talk to you later.''

''Yeah, later—and I am *not* cranky in the morning!'' Disgruntled, Meredith hung up the phone. Avoiding Cal would be difficult with Ellen calling up to arrange appointments.

She showered, dressed, then ate breakfast without appetite. Kayanne arrived a short time later, looking as if she'd lost her last friend.

''What is it, Kayanne? Nothing's wrong with the new apartment, is there?'' Meredith asked, with suspended breath. During her first year at Dallas Art School, Kayanne had stayed with her, but when they landed the Lipscomb account Kayanne had felt solvent enough to strike out on her own. She'd been in her new apartment two days, and as much as Meredith loved her baby sister she had welcomed that new arrangement.

She tried not to look as relieved as she felt when Kayanne said, ''No, Mere. It's nothing like that. It's Mrs. Lipscomb. Would you believe that old cow has decided to go Japanese?''

''Kayanne, we don't refer to our clients as 'old cows,' '' Meredith informed her distraught sister. ''Suppose you tell me all about it.''

''What's to tell?'' Kayanne muttered as she plopped down on the white living-room sofa. ''It's like I said. That old . . . Mrs. Lipscomb wants Japanese. Can you believe it, Mere? I mean, Japanese in a historic Swiss Avenue house? And after she had us do the place in French antiques. Now she's bound and determined to have nothing but cushions. I'm serious, Mere. She wants nothing but cushions and pillows. That old . . . that woman has to weigh three hundred pounds, at least. Can you imagine her sitting on floor cushions?''

"I'm trying to imagine her getting up again," Meredith said, laughing.

Kayanne was not amused. "It's not funny, Mere. Pillows means her tables can't be higher than sixteen inches. What in the Sam Hill am I suppose to do with the ones we ordered? Chop off the legs?" Kayanne sounded on the verge of tears. She had recently turned twenty, and looked even younger than that today. Her green eyes were big in her pale face, her shining red hair swung in a ponytail, and her chin was beginning to quiver. Meredith resisted the urge to comfort and protect the baby chick. Kayanne was unsure of her own abilities, but she had more than enough talent to become a full partner in the business someday.

"Calm down," Meredith said in her most authoritive yet sisterly soothing voice. "Everything's going to be fine."

"I don't know how. Mrs. Lipscomb insists that it's all our fault, the tables being too tall. She won't pay the balance on her account."

Meredith chewed on her thumbnail. That wasn't good news. Not coming after all the money she'd spent lately on the House of the Seasons. It was her practice to give clients a complete estimate of what a job would cost, including everything from the price of new draperies to the fee for her time and expertise. She generally requested one-half the amount in advance, an arrangement that usually gave her satisfactory working capital until the job was completed. But Cal's house was different. It had needs she could not even have imagined in the beginning. Needs she could learn only as she reacquainted herself with the house's gracious spirit. That meant she was using the deposit Cal had given her daddy much faster than she'd expected.

Reminding herself firmly that all her purchases and repairs so far had been necessary, Meredith sat down beside her sister. Somehow everything would work out. ''Just relax,'' she told Kayanne. ''I know you can handle Mrs. Lipscomb. And we agreed you should have more responsibility, right?''

''Sure, but not this much! Mrs. Lipscomb's house has twenty-five rooms, Mere. It's the biggest account we've ever had, and I'm afraid we're going to lose it!''

''Bite your tongue.'' Meredith sighed. ''Positive, Kayanne. We have to think positive. That's what it takes to survive in this business, or any business, for that matter.''

Kayanne took a deep breath, then let it out slowly through pursed lips; she sounded like a balloon deflating. ''Somehow I don't think a positive attitude is enough this time, Mere. The problem is, you're becoming obsessed with the House of the Seasons, and you're leaving me in the lurch with Mrs. Lipscomb.''

Kayanne was right, unfortunately. Meredith wasn't interested in decorating any other house except Cal's at the moment. She loved the House of the Seasons. It was as simple as that.

''Tell you what,'' Meredith said. ''You take Mrs. Lipscomb to lunch today, and then shopping. Buy her a short table or two. Let her live with them for a few days. She's bound to reconsider.''

''I don't know, Mere,'' Kayanne said, shaking her head.

''Don't worry,'' Meredith said encouragingly. ''I have faith in you, baby sister, and I'll come by tonight and have a talk with Mrs. Lipscomb myself.''

''Promise?''

''I promise. Now, we'd both better get it in gear. I'm

going to Crystal Creek to work on the house for a while.''

Even working on the house did not help Meredith's mood. Her sense of contentment was gone, replaced by a restless unease. The atmosphere was still charged after the way Cal had kissed her last night. By the time she left to keep her appointment her insides had twisted into one big, apprehensive knot.

The Diamond Club was located in The Ballpark in Arlington, home of the Texas Rangers baseball team. It was a state-of-the-art building with the utmost in customer convenience. Yet the ballpark was designed and built with tradition and intimacy in mind, containing features such as granite and brick facades, exposed structural steel, an asymmetrical playing field, and a home run porch in right field. Texas architecture was featured throughout, from the outer facade to the Lone Stars in the concourses and on the seat aisles.

Each of the parking lots was named after a Texas hero. Naturally, the ones for season ticket holders were closest to the park; they also carried a thousand-dollar annual fee. Meredith loved baseball, and she and Kayanne and Bo attended as many Rangers home games as they had time for and could afford each season. The home run porch seats were reasonably priced, although parking in one of the public lots constituted a lengthy hike to the stadium.

This time she left her van in the reserved Davy Crockett Lot, like any other VIP.

The Diamond Club, located in left field, was also for the pleasure of season ticket holders. A great place to enjoy a power lunch or elegant dinner while watching a baseball game . . . for those with discriminating taste and the money to indulge those whims. The view of the playing field was spectacular, even with the Rangers on the road.

Meredith glanced around at the four tiers of seating— a lofty perch for the privileged. Most of the patrons wore drab business suits.

Meredith nonchalantly straightened the collar of her flowered shirt, and tucked one hand into the pocket of her navy pants, clutching her briefcase with the other. She felt out of place here, but she certainly wasn't going to show it.

Then she saw Cal. He was just rising from a front row table, shaking hands with two men outfitted in somber suits. There was nothing drab about Cal Bonner. His navy-and-taupe sportcoat was the kind of jacket that would look great with jeans on Friday or dress slacks on Monday, and his vigorous good looks hinted at the untamed. As the two men walked away, Cal turned to scan the restaurant. His eyes locked with Meredith's, and she suddenly seemed to have forgotten how to walk across a room. Cal wasn't any help; he just stood there, looking at her intently without smiling or even nodding an acknowledgment. At last she was able to put one foot in front of the other, propelling herself toward him.

"Hello, Cal," she said as breezily as possible.

"Thank you for coming, Meredith," he answered, his tone formal. "I had a business meeting here and thought it might be a good idea if you and I met here, on neutral ground." He stood beside her as she slid into the chair he'd pulled out, his hand brushing her shoulder. She was left with a warm, tingling sensation.

He sat across from her. "Would you like something to eat or drink?" he asked, the gravity of his expression relaxing slightly as he watched her.

"I'll have iced tea, thank you. With lemon."

His expression relaxed still further, almost into a smile, and he ordered two iced teas with lemon. Meredith pulled her notepad from the briefcase, ready with her pencil. But Cal leaned back, apparently in no hurry to explain the purpose of the meeting. Meredith found herself gazing at his generous, expressive mouth, her senses remembering that kiss.

"I didn't realize you were a season ticket holder," she said, mostly to make converation.

"I'm not. Sunmedia pays the tab. Clients seem to enjoy the perks."

"Clients?" Meredith couldn't help smiling. "For Sunmedia, I'm sure you're right, but the *Chronicle* isn't exactly the Dallas *Morning News.* I can't imagine anybody in the metroplex wanting to advertise in a small-town weekly."

Cal looked smugly pleased with himself. "Those two men who just left here did. One owns several auto parts stores. The other just opened his tenth area miniature golf course. Both bought space in the *Chronicle.*"

"Really," Meredith said with appropriate awe. "I am impressed, Mr. Bonner. You must be some kind of salesman. To my knowledge there's never been metroplex advertising in the *Chronicle* before."

"It's called motivation. My father expects the *Chronicle* to show a profit, and it's my ticket back to civilization."

Meredith gave him a long, hard look. "You're talking about my hometown, Mr. Bonner."

"And you're taking everything personally again, Ms. Grant. I have nothing against Crystal Creek. It's just not for me. And I don't see you living there, either. But that's beside the point. The reason I asked you to meet me here is that I bought something for the house."

"Oh?" Meredith answered distractedly, hanging on to her notepad.

"Yes. I'd like to show it to you." He produced a roll of paper from the seat beside him and spread it out on the table in front of Meredith.

It was a print of H. W. Caylor's *The Chuckwagon.* She contemplated the subtle contrast of land and sky, the cowboys and horses. After a long moment she looked up and gave Cal a beneficent smile. The knot inside her was slowly beginning to unravel.

"This is wonderful," she said. "I can have it framed—and I think one of the upstairs rooms would be perfect for it."

"Good," he said, rolling it up again.

"I didn't know you were interested in art."

"Why does that surprise you?"

"I don't know. The problem is, I don't really know you at all." She found herself gazing at his mouth again, and had to avert her eyes. "What I meant is that I try to have an idea of my client's personalities. The house should reflect you . . ." Meredith paused, forehead wrinkled in perplexity.

"I'm glad you find the idea so appealing," he said sardonically.

"You don't understand. It's just that I don't have you figured out yet. Are you the white wall type, or Caylor-on-the-walls?"

He gave her a slow grin. "Maybe I'm both. Maybe people aren't as easy to catalog as wallpaper samples."

"I'm not trying to catalog you," she protested. "I'm just trying to do my job. And I can't do it if you won't give me at least a little insight about yourself. Why don't you begin by telling me about your taste in art?"

"That's not exactly something you just spit out for

social conversation. Show me a painting. I'll tell you if I like it.''

Why did everything have to be so difficult with this man? She tried again. "You must know if you hate Renoir, or if Cézanne is your favorite, or Frans Hals . . .''

"I'm open to anything.''

Meredith drew a jagged line across her pad. First he wanted plain white walls, now he was "open to anything.'' "Okay,'' she said. "Let's narrow that down a bit. What sort of house did you grow up in? What did you like about it? What didn't you like?''

He shrugged, and settled back with his frosted glass of iced tea, his eyes enigmatic. But at last he began. "Bonners don't grow up in houses, Meredith. We have mansions and estates. The one in Highland Park has seven . . . no, eight bedrooms, and nine bathrooms. The country estate only has five of each, plus a rustic log cabin for guests, and stables for horses. I suppose my favorite is the farm in the wine district of Charente. The house is big and drafty, but it felt like home, somehow. Have you ever been to France?''

"No.''

"I think you'd like it.''

There was suddenly a silence between them, strained and uncomfortable. Meredith sipped her tea, but couldn't think of a thing to say.

"Why did you decide to be an interior designer?'' Cal asked.

"It's something I always wanted, I suppose. I have five brothers and sisters, so my mom didn't have the time or the energy to make our home pretty. I was the one trying to figure out how to make cheap curtains look better, or how to use Contact paper on the refrigerator so it wouldn't look quite so shabby. And we only had one house, and one bathroom, which you could never use when you wanted to.'' She stopped, hesitant to reveal too much about herself. ''So . . . how did you end up running a small-town weekly? It obviously wasn't your idea.''

He gazed at her thoughtfully, taking a moment to answer. ''My parents weren't a good match. She's poetic and he's eccentric, and their only child turned out to be a degenerate.''

''Excuse me?''

''That's what passes for humor in the Bonner family.'' He propped his elbows on the table. ''I was a pretty wild kid, I guess, and my father thinks I'm lingering in my collegiate years. He's determined for me to reach my chronological age of twenty-nine, if it kills us both, and I'm sure it's less complicated to be a steady guy. I'm just not sure how that's done. But to make a long and exceedingly boring story short, I'm in Crystal Creek to learn the business from the 'gound up,' to quote my father. And because he has no sense of humor where two thousand dollars' worth of speeding tickets and two wrecked company cars are concerned.''

''You did that? Are you . . . uh . . . I mean, do you party a lot?''

He gave her a long, serious, significant look. ''You mean do I make a habit of drinking and driving, and the answer is no. I'm no angel, and I admit to an addiction to fast cars. That might make me irresponsible, but I'm not stupid. I don't drink and drive, Meredith. In fact, I never touch anything stronger than Pepsi . . . oh, and coffee.''

''And you're stuck in the boondocks until the *Chronicle* turns a profit,'' Meredith supplied.

''Something like that.''

"So why did you buy the House of the Seasons if you don't intend to stay?"

His expression suggested she lacked some fundamental marbles. "Where was I going to live? The bus station? If your hometown has any apartment complexes I must have missed them."

"There isn't a bus station, either. But I get your point. And it's back to big D as soon as possible?"

Cal shook his head. "Sunmedia is expanding to France. I've got my airplane ticket on hold."

Why on earth did that bother her? Her reaction was disturbing, to say the least. She ought to feel relieved that he was planning on leaving the country. She dropped her unused notepad back into her briefcase, trying to act as businesslike as possible. "I really should be going."

"Meredith, you know we have to talk about it. Our kiss last night." He said the words so matter-of-factly Meredith stiffened.

"Really, Cal, there's nothing to talk about." She knew she had failed miserably in her attempt to sound casual. She clutched her briefcase.

"I think there is." He ran a hand over the veneer of the tabletop. "I wanted to apologize for what happened. It was a mistake. I think we both realize that."

Meredith nibbled on her bottom lip. He didn't have to be *quite* so apologetic. He was right, though; she did agree that the whole thing was a mistake.

"It won't happen again," she said. "It was unprofessional."

"I'm glad you see it the same way."

"It's never a good idea to become involved with a business associate." Meredith relaxed her hold on the briefcase. "Besides, I enjoy my life as it is, and I'm not looking to get involved with anyone. I'm a very independent person.''

"So I've noticed," he said wryly.

"A woman has to be," she declared. "Take my mother, for instance. She adores my father, but he has old-fashioned notions and ideas, which translate into domineering, intentional or not. He manages her, just like she was one of his kids. She doesn't see it that way, unfortunately."

"I take it he doesn't manage you too well."

"We've had our moments," Meredith admitted. "When I first moved away he installed new safety locks on all my doors—you know, protection in the big city. The locks don't always work, however. I remember him saying that if I had a man around I wouldn't have that problem. I told him that I did have a man around, and he was the problem. He cares for me, though, a lot, and he's a wonderful man. He brings my mother violets at least once a month, and I still have those locks."

Cal smiled at her. She felt a pleasurable warmth seeping through her. She liked being able to speak so frankly with him.

"So . . . I didn't want you to have any bad feelings about last night," he said.

"I don't. Not anymore. I'm glad we cleared the air. I really am."

"It won't happen again."

"You can count on that."

They gazed at each other. Meredith broke the eye contact first, to glance at her watch. "I do have to be going."

They stood at the same time. Cal paid the tab and escorted her outside. "I'm in the Davy Crockett Lot," she said. "What about you?"

"At the moment, I'm on foot. I was just debating if it would be unprofessional of me to ask for a lift."

"Where's your car?"

"In the shop for maintenance. They dropped me off here, but they didn't have a loaner available. I figured I'd take a taxi home."

"All the way to Crystal Creek?" He nodded. Meredith laughed and said, "Boy, you *are* rich. Come on, I'll give you a ride. Anything to keep a client happy." She was feeling very kind toward him now that everything was straightened out between them.

"Are you sure? I don't want to be any trouble."

"You aren't. I have some things in the van I needed to drop off at your house, anyway."

"I appreciate this, Meredith. I'm due at a fund-raiser tonight and a friend is picking me up." He rubbed his neck. "I'm not looking forward to it, but I'll do anything to snare more advertisers."

"Anything within reason," Meredith contributed, and they both laughed.

Fortunately, all her workers had left on schedule, so Cal would have the house to himself. But he seemed in a generous mood as he climbed out of the van and came around to lean in her window.

"I'll help you unload this stuff," he said. "And since I'll be gone tonight, I won't mind if you stay and wreak havoc on the house."

"Why, thank you, Cal. And you'll be pleased with the end results. I promise." Now Meredith felt a sense of camaraderie with Cal as the two of them lugged boxes into the storage room behind the kitchen. After that task was finished he went upstairs and Meredith decided to tackle the awkward section of wallpapering in the hall.

She had chosen a pattern of violets and couldn't wait to see what it would look like.

The noise of the shower running carried down to her as she puttered about. It was far too intimate a sound, and she tried to blank it out from her mind. She clambered up on the stepladder. It wasn't tall enough; she had to stretch up on the very tips of her toes in order to reach any corners.

When Cal came downstairs, he was dressed in a tuxedo, which contrasted against his blond hair and emphasized the clean lines of his features. The jacket was cut perfectly to the breadth of his shoulders. Definitely not a rental.

Meredith found herself gaping at him. Before she knew it, she had teetered too far on the edge of the ladder. She came crashing down, helplessly raking her fingers against the plaster for a hold.

Cal was beside her in an instant, kneeling down to extricate her from the rolls of wallpaper. ''Have you broken anything?''

''No . . . ouch!''

''What is it?''

''I was wrong. I did break something. A nail.'' She nursed the jagged edge of it, trying to scoot away from him. ''Look out, you'll get dirty.''

''Don't be absurd.'' He took her elbow and managed to raise her to her feet. ''Let's see your finger.''

''It's just a nail, for crying out loud.''

''Let me see it.''

Unwillingly she gave him her hand. She stared at his immaculate white shirt front and fought an overwhelming urge to nestle her dirt-smudged face against it. Her head moved imperceptibly yet dangerously closer to Cal's chest. He ran his fingers gently over her cheek.

It was just a breath of a touch, and yet it made her knees weak.

"Meredith," he murmured.

"You don't have to ply me with sweet talk. I'm not going to sue." Her voice came shakily.

His chuckle was low and deep, sending a shivery warmth down her spine.

"You have a marvelous sense of humor, Meredith," he said, his mouth close to her ear. "I just wish I could figure you out. You're a complete mystery to me."

"I'm not mysterious . . . I'm . . . sensible . . . completely sensible . . ." She closed her eyes, drawing in her breath as his rough-soft cheek moved against hers.

He held her for another moment, then released her slowly. "I'm sorry, Meredith. I did promise this wouldn't happen again."

Meredith trembled, feeling empty with Cal's arms no longer around her. "No problem," she said, smoothing back her hair.

"I'm glad you're not angry."

"Why should I be angry?" she snapped.

Cal regarded her. "Because you're not the kind of woman who can be casual about a kiss," he said. "That's a refreshing quality. Don't try to hide it."

She lifted her chin defiantly. "I'm not trying to hide anything. We're business associates. We should avoid . . . certain things. But one kiss is nothing to get worked up about." She folded her arms tightly, willing her heart to stop its tumult. She was angry all right—at herself! How could she respond so quickly to this man's touch?

The knocker at the front door rapped peremptorily, jarring Meredith's taut nerves.

"That must be my ride," Cal said. "Be careful tonight, Meredith. Don't kill yourself on that ladder."

"I'm perfectly capable of taking care of myself," she retorted. His expression was skeptical as he went to open the door.

A beautiful woman stood on the porch. No, she wasn't just beautiful; riveting was a more appropriate word to describe her. Luxuriant silver-blond hair cascaded over her bare shoulders; her mouth was an unabashed slash of scarlet in a cream-white face. Every curve of her stunning figure was tightly sheathed in green silk.

"Hello, Cal," the woman purred, giving him a frank appraisal. "You're looking better than ever. It has been a while. That's why I volunteered to be your chauffeur tonight." She made "chauffeur" sound like something delightfully wicked, and her eyes roved over Cal as if he were a double-dip ice-cream cone. Meredith glanced at him to gage his reaction to the female admiration. It was impossible to tell what he was thinking. Women probably looked at him like that all the time. Meredith herself looked at him like that. It was a perfectly natural and perfectly annoying reaction!

"Cynthia Campbell, I'd like you to meet Meredith Grant," Cal was saying. Cynthia Campbell barely flicked a glance in Meredith's direction. She tucked her hand in the crook of Cal's arm, her long crimson fingernails resplendent against his tuxedo.

"Come on, Cal," she said in her throaty voice. "We're already late."

Cal started to look over his shoulder at Meredith, but Cynthia Campbell proved she had muscle along with everything else as she squired Cal away.

Meredith shut the door after them, leaning her forehead against it. The emptiness inside her was filling with a sharp pain whose source she didn't understand. It shouldn't bother her that Cal was spending the evening with a beautiful woman. He and Meredith had agreed that their relationship ought to remain a strictly professional one—which didn't include room for jealousy.

Meredith hated herself for what she did next. She simply could not stop from running up to the landing windows. She was just in time to see Cynthia and Cal driving away in a sleek silver BMW roadster convertible. Meredith's nine-year-old dirty blue van looked dowdy and forlorn as the BMW swept past it.

She wilted and sank onto the stairway, rubbing her hand across her dirty cheek. But after a moment she sat up straight and glanced about defiantly into the gathering dusk. She could go out tonight herself, if she wanted to. She did have one really fantastic evening gown, and there was always Dale. So what if Dale Hanson was just a family friend, a boy she'd grown up with and who was like one of her brothers?

She wrapped her arms around her knees and wondered if Cynthia Campbell was Cal's Dale Hanson, so to speak. Somehow the thought didn't cheer her up. She couldn't see Cynthia as anybody's sister, much less Cal's.

She took a rag and started rubbing grime away from the newel post. But she couldn't concentrate on anything. All she could think about was Cal dancing close to Cynthia in a ballroom somewhere. The thought was torment.

She threw down the rag. There was no peace here tonight. She had to get out . . . and she did promise Kayanne that she'd go over to Mrs. Lipscomb's and discuss short tables. That was exactly what she'd do.

Meredith snatched up her briefcase and escaped.

Chapter Four

Reunion Tower shimmered in the mirror glass of a downtown office building. It was a spectacular view of that huge ball on stilts, the giant dotted "i" that punctuated Dallas's skyline. The sun was shinning bright and clear, and Meredith should have been in the best of spirits, for it was Saturday, the best day of the week, and she was out in the fresh air. Yet as she wandered along a West End street, all she could think about was Cal and Cynthia Campbell—and that was ruining what should have been a perfect day.

It maddened Meredith that she couldn't stop wondering how Cal had spent last evening. She longed to be as carefree and independent of heart as she'd always been before, with no man disturbing her happiness. No unwanted emotions.

She trudged on aimlessly. But then a Tiffany floral lamp gleamed at her from one of the shop windows. It would be perfect for Cal's library. Meredith walked into the store with a sense of purpose. She was beginning to feel a little better.

The lamp was an original Louis C. Tiffany design, probably a century old, and it was expensive. Very expensive. But it was an exquisite lamp, hand-rolled art glass that was individually cut, copper foiled, and leaded into a multicolor "Roses" design. The cast-metal base had an antiqued bronze finish. The House of the Seasons needed something exactly like this, even though it wasn't in the original budget. Meredith opened her checkbook to give its contents a hopeful perusal.

Her optimism was ill-founded. She had written quite a few checks lately for Cal's house, and had jotted the figures down hastily without subtracting them from her bank balance. She did some mental calculations and winced at the results. She stuffed the checkbook back into her briefcase and fished for a credit card instead.

The sales associate drifted away for a few minutes, then drifted back again. "Denied," he said in a pale, expressionless voice that matched his pale, expressionless face.

Meredith straightened up from her examination of a cast and handpainted collectible 1900s circus wagon. "Excuse me?"

"Credit card denied."

"That's impossible."

"Nothing's impossible."

"Good grief. Well . . . wait a minute, please." Meredith swung her briefcase up onto the counter and snapped it open in a businesslike fashion. She started rummaging through her lipstick, compact, hand lotion, keys, spare packets of tissues, the travel sewing kit she'd thought she had lost.

The sales associate, a fortyish man with a head as bald as an egg, leaned over the counter to observe. Meredith drew her eyebrows together. Angling the briefcase to block his view, she went on hunting. She pushed aside some spare change and a few tea bags and packets of jelly. There it was—her other credit card. She handed it crisply to the sales associate.

This time she followed him. She hovered about as he passed her card through the obnoxious machine.

"Also denied." The card came shooting back to her. She glanced suspiciously at the machine.

"There must be some mistake."

The clerk shook his head. He was beginning to look quite alert, and slightly amused. "Want to try another one?"

"I think that's enough, thank you." She turned and snapped her briefcase shut.

"You know what they say," the clerk remarked in a deadpan voice. "Third time's a charm."

Meredith felt totally flustered. She gazed at the lamp. This was awful, just awful. She could have sworn she was nowhere near her credit limit.

The sales associate was giving her a mild yet relentless stare. She retreated outside, and this time she didn't look in any shop windows as she hurried down the street. Cal's deposit money was gone, and she still had so much to do for the house. She'd already started the carpenters building cabinets and shelves, and they would be expecting payment soon. Things weren't going well with Mrs. Lipscomb, either; last night's discussion about short tables had not been a success. Mrs. Lipscomb had stared at her with a dour expression, like a latter-day Queen Victoria enthroned on cushions. Meredith had tried referring gently to the woman's arthritis, which acted up from time to time in the summer humidity; surely chairs and ordinary tables would be less of a strain. Mrs. Lipscomb had remained adamant. She wanted a Japanese motif, and Meredith had gone home with leg cramps from sitting on a pillow.

Now she headed for her van. Everything was getting out of hand. Yet the only solution she could think of at the moment was to retreat to Crystal Creek. She'd have the house to herself, and perhaps the solitude would inspire her.

When she arrived, however, she found that Cal's Jaguar was back from the shop and parked in the driveway. She pulled up beside it, grateful not to see any silver BMWs.

She had been able to make at least one purchase this morning—two cans of paint stripper. She began lugging them toward the porch. A bee buzzed lazily past her into the garden, distracting her for a moment. Weeds had taken over the flower beds; only a few hardy rosebushes still flourished, growing wild now. The marble fountain was mournfully dry, with a ceramic frog in its center. She'd have to do something about all this neglect. Everywhere she turned, another part of the house begged for her attention. Somehow she had to find enough money to provide the right care.

Her arms were aching as she toiled up the steps of the porch. The front door swung open in front of her, and there was Cal. Her eyes began at the toes of his running shoes, traveled up the lean length of his jean-clad legs, and stopped at the faded blue cotton that strained across his shoulders.

"On your way out?" she asked hopefully to his chest as she backed away.

"No, I'm not." He took the heavy cans from her and set them inside the door.

"Ellen said you'd be working at the newspaper all weekend."

"I changed my mind."

"I see." Meredith straightened a crease on her jeans. "I hope you had a good time at your fund-raiser last night," she said insincerely.

"It was okay," he said. "Nothing special. I lined up a couple of new accounts and then had Cynthia bring me home early."

"I see." *Good grief,* Meredith berated herself. Couldn't she think of anything else to say? But her heart was lightened by the knowledge that Cynthia Campbell had not completely dazzled Cal. She found herself grinning foolishly at him.

"Where are those shutters that need hanging?" he asked.

"What?"

"Shutters. You know, those things you hang outside windows."

"I know what shutters are, but you're not supposed to do any work on the house," Meredith protested.

"It's my house. If I want to hang shutters, that's what I'll do."

"I didn't mean it that way," she said, poking her sneaker at a pile of old boards. "I mean, if you want to work on the house, fine. But you don't have to. I take full responsibility for the job I set out for myself—"

"Meredith," Cal said with a sigh, "where are the shutters?"

An hour later Meredith sat back from stripping the wainscoting in the library, glad to see that she was right about it. The natural grain was going to look beautiful in here, just as she remembered it. She stood up and stretched, gratified at how easy it was to work with Cal close by. She went to the window, listening to the cheerful sound of nails being hammered into wood. Equally cheery was the sound of whistling. Cal Bonner whistling? Meredith smiled. Her financial problems were beginning to fade into the background. As a child, this house had been her magical dream conduit. Not much had changed. She resumed stripping paint.

She was deeply engrossed when Cal poked his head inside the room. "Lunch is served," he announced. "Meet me in the kitchen in five minutes." He disappeared before she could say anything. Mystified, she cleaned up in the small bathroom located beneath the stairs and went to see what he was concocting.

It turned out to be a giant, impressive-looking omelet. Meredith breathed in the aroma of onions and chives.

"I didn't know you could cook," she said, taking two plates from the cupboard. "That smells wonderful."

"I have a few surprises up my sleeve," he said.

"I'll vouch for that," she returned, opening the drawer where the plastic forks and spoons were kept. Here was another surprise already—the plastic had been replaced by a set of stainless-steel flatware. She picked up a spoon and examined it critically. Nothing fancy, but certainly serviceable. She nodded, only to glance over and find Cal watching her sardonically.

"I'm glad you're finally settling in," she said.

"You didn't even notice the new drain board. You're slipping, Ms. Grant."

"It's a wonderful tray," she pronounced. "But didn't they have it in any color besides putrid green?"

"Will you stop trying to color-coordinate my life?" he grumbled.

"No," Meredith said happily. The best surprise today was how comfortable she felt with Cal. She sat down with him and they shared their meal in companionable silence. The omelet was delicious.

"Who taught you to cook like this?" she asked, leaning back luxuriously. "Your mother?"

Cal laughed. "Hardly. Sodie is poetic, and she's an

excellent hostess, but I'm not sure she's ever seen the inside of a kitchen before.''

''Sodie? That's an unusual name.''

''She's an unusual woman. Actually, her name is Sarah, but everybody calls her Sodie. Don't ask me why, because I have no idea.''

''Okay, I won't ask. But if your mother didn't teach you how to cook, who did?''

''A French governess who raised me, for all practical purposes. Suzanne Glemet. I spent every summer with her on our Charente farm. I was supposed to be perfecting my French, and Miss Suzanne took me to all the studios and galleries in Paris. And she was also a gourmet cook.''

''She sounds interesting.'' Meredith propped her elbows on the table, while Cal regarded his plate thoughtfully.

''She . . . was,'' he finally replied. ''She passed away a couple of years ago. I haven't been able to go back to that farmhouse since. Miss Suzanne had a passion for art. She collected Soutine and Munch long before they were big names in art, and she probably never paid much more than a hundred dollars for any of their works. She bought her first painting when she was sixteen. A Dufy. For fifty dollars. She adored Dufy, for she had his kind of spirit. She could be bowled over by color. That's why she loved the Impressionists so. Her favorite painting was Dufy's *Pink Lady*. But she didn't spend all her time visiting the Louvre. She was on the French Olympic ski team back in the forties, and we spent a lot of time together on the slopes of the Alps.''

Meredith was listening intently. ''You *have* led an interesting life. Or maybe exotic is a better word. Paris. Skiing in the Alps. The Grant bunch spent our summers at a Baptist camp and an adventure was a trip over to Six Flags. I've never even been on a pair of skis.''

"You should try it. You'd love skiing.''

Meredith shivered, just thinking about the cold and the snow and ice. "Actually, I do really well in the lodge. My sister Joleen and her husband, Travis, talked me into going with them to Colorado one Christmas. I spent the entire time reading a book and drinking hot chocolate. Joleen broke her leg.''

"I'd get you out on the slopes first thing,'' he said. "You'd like it.''

"No, I wouldn't,'' she said stubbornly. "I don't like snow and I don't like cold, and I'm not crazy about the idea of a broken leg. This is Princess Klutz you're talking to, remember?''

"How do you know you wouldn't like it if you haven't tried it?'' he persisted.

"I've never jumped off a cliff, either, but I can say with certainty I wouldn't like it. And skiing isn't my idea of fun, either. Okay?''

He was leaning toward her. "You're being very narrow-minded, Meredith. That surprises me.''

She glared at him. "Maybe you're just too accustomed to having everything your way and getting everything you want, and a woman with her own interests is too much for you.''

"How did you jump to that conclusion?'' He glared back at her. "I just happen to think people should be willing to try new things.''

"What if I tried it?'' she asked guardedly. "What if I tried skiing and I didn't like it? What would you say then?''

"I'd say you didn't give it enough of a chance.''

Her fork clattered down on her plate. "Talk about

narrow-minded,'' she said in disgust. ''You think a woman should want to do everything you do.''

''Listen, I grew up with parents who didn't have a thing in common. Two people need to share interests.''

''As long as they're the man's, right?'' she taunted him.

''I didn't say that.''

''You didn't have to . . . and haven't you heard the saying 'variety is the spice of life'?'' She gathered up the plates with a great deal more clatter. ''Cynthia Campbell probably skis,'' she muttered, and was instantly sorry she had spoken the words aloud.

''As a matter of fact, she does,'' Cal said. ''And when I see her tonight I'll be sure and mention that you asked about her.''

''Fine.'' Meredith stood at the counter, battling a wretched wave of jealousy.

''She's having a dinner party for some people she does business with. She thought it would be an excellent opportunity for me to sell more advertising.''

''It's no concern of mine how or when you see Cynthia Campbell,'' Meredith said stiffly. ''I don't know why you feel the need to explain anything to me.''

''I don't know why, either. But there you have it.''

Meredith swiped at crumbs on the counter with a paper towel. A wayward image crept into her mind: she and Cal bundled up in mittens and mufflers, out on a snowy French mountaintop together . . . just the two of them.

That was the frightening thing. Even though she knew she'd hate skiing, part of her longed to go out there and make herself cold and miserable. Just so she could be on that mountaintop with Cal. Just so she could be his type of woman over all the Cynthia Campbells of the world. And there would go Meredith Grant, the independent person she'd fought so hard to become. Yes, it was frightening, wanting so badly to please a man.

She pushed the plates across the counter. No way was she going anywhere near that sink today. It was far too dangerous.

''I'll get back to work,'' she said briskly. ''Thanks for lunch.''

''My pleasure,'' Cal said, but his tone didn't agree with the message. He went back outside, and the pounding of nails sounded more vigorous than necessary. The whistling had stopped.

Meredith took several turns around the library, wondering just how ''friendly'' a friend Cynthia Campbell was to Cal. She certainly hadn't wasted any time arranging another evening with him, and perhaps this time she'd be more successful renewing their friendship—or whatever the heck had been between them!

''She can have him!'' Meredith declared to the empty room. Even to her the words didn't sound very convincing. She stalked upstairs to look for anything that would make her stop brooding about Cal and Cynthia.

She paused in a doorway, examining the ratty green carpet she'd started to pull up. This was the room where she planned to hang Cal's print once it was framed. Whenever she saw a painting by Caylor she would think of Cal.

This wasn't doing her any good. Turning, Meredith opened the door across the hall. She saw a pair of loafers discarded carelessly on the rag rug, a shirt tossed across the back of a chair. Cal's bedroom. Meredith hestitated, then stepped inside. There was only the barest amount of furniture—the chair, bed, nightstand, chest. She picked up the book that was open facedown on the night-

stand and read the title: *You Can't Go Home Again.*
Thomas Wolfe—that seemed right for Cal. She glanced
down, eyes lingering on the rumpled sheets of his bed.
His pillow had been twisted and punched up against the
wall, as if he, too, had spent a restless night.

She moved her hand over the pillow, thinking of his
tousled head pressed against it. She could easily imagine
his powerful body lying there, tense with energy even in
sleep. Her hand crept downward, fingering a corner of
the sheet . . .

What in the Sam Hill had come over her? She straightened quickly and backed away. She turned and fled the
room, retreating all the way to the attic.

Here at last she found something to occupy her mind.
She began poking about among all the boxes. This mess
really did need to be cleared out, and yet the place would
lose much of its atmosphere all neat and bare. Attics
were meant for treasures like this. Maybe that was why
the local historical committee had left them here.

She found hundred-year-old recipes, mildewed books,
a moth-eaten scarf, and faded photographs of children
playing along the banks of a creek. Meredith settled
down cross-legged and pored over the photographs.
Young faces laughed up at her, their happiness shining
even through the cracked, yellowed film of age. Children
who had grown up in this house. One of them was probably Ima Benjamine, the house's last resident. Meredith
wondered if Ima had loved the House of the Seasons as
much as she did.

She put the photos back in their shoe box, but couldn't
resist scavenging through a big chest pushed against one
wall. It was filled with old dresses, the cloth thin and
brittle under her fingers.

"Oh, my goodness," she breathed, holding up a swirl

of polka dots, then a froth of yellowed lace. Perhaps Miss Ima had worn these dresses to garden parties or leisurely afternoon teas. And here was a gown that surely had been worn to a ball. It was simple yet strikingly elegant, an off-the-shoulder lavender silk with a full skirt swirling to the floor.

Meredith held it gently against her body, closing her eyes and humming a waltz to herself. She could see a string orchestra playing in a ballroom where couples skimmed over the parquet floors. Unbidden, an image of Cal popped into her mind, the way he had looked last night in his tuxedo. He fit too easily into her fantasy; it was too easy to imagine him clasping her hand in his and leading her out onto the dance floor. He pulled her close, his cheek resting against her hair.

Meredith hummed her waltz louder, with a deliberately martial beat; that didn't stop the Cal in her dream from drawing her still closer.

"You look beautiful," he said huskily.

Meredith froze, her eyes flew open. Cal was sitting next to the trapdoor, gazing at her intently. The blood rushed to her face, and she lost her grip on the dress. It floated down to the dusty floorboards. She grappled for it, but in one easy motion Cal stood and was beside her. He rescued the dress, brushed it off, and handed it back to her. The ceiling was so low that he had to lean over her. Meredith took a deep, shuddering breath, and the next second she was in Cal's arms, the dress crushed against her.

"No . . . please . . ." she whispered. Her words were lost as his mouth descended hungrily to hers. No fantasy could have captured the actual feel of him—the searing pressure of his lips, the lean, hard strength of his body. Fire coursed through her in response, sweeping away all her defenses. Her hands moved upward over his shoulders. His muscles tightened under her touch, and he gave a low groan. The silk rustled between them, unheeded.

Her body fit so closely against him, and she longed to be closer. The need in her was overwhelming, more terrifying than any sensation she had ever known. She felt powerless against it. Her lips melted willingly into his. He tasted fresh and warm and clean.

Then he broke away from her, and the attic suddenly seemed cold, despite its stuffy air. They were both breathing raggedly. Meredith held the gown against her as if for protection.

"That shouldn't have happened," Cal said.

"No," she agreed woodenly, not understanding how fire could bank down so suddenly to ashes.

"You'll have to forgive me—and forget about it."

It was already too late for that. She knew that she would always remember the feel and the taste of him.

"I suppose that will be easy for you," she blurted. "To forget you came up here and—"

"Nothing is easy with you, Meredith," he said roughly. His eyes had darkened with some emotion she could not fathom. She turned away, clutching the dress still tighter.

"You're the one making everything so difficult," she muttered. "You weren't supposed to be here today."

"You're right. I don't know what the devil I'm doing here. I've got a pile of work waiting for me at the newspaper. That's where I should have been in the first place." He left her abruptly.

Meredith felt raw inside. She slowly loosened her grip on the poor gown, making a futile attempt to smooth out the wrinkles. It still felt warm from the contact with Cal. She returned it to the old chest, then sank down and rested her forehead against her knees. She was completely drained, completely shaken. How foolish it was to daydream, to imagine a perfect romantic scene. Because the reality was far too dangerous, pushing her to acknowledge feelings better left ignored.

Yet how could she deny the sensations Cal aroused in her? They were not merely physical. That she could have dealt with—explained away as normal responses of a healthy body. What Cal made her feel . . .

She straightened, rubbing her temples. This feeling went too deep, touching some place inside her that she'd never known existed before. And then to suffer the coldness, the hurt when he withdrew his arms, to wonder about the woman he'd be seeing tonight . . .

She scrambled to her feet. She had let this get out of hand, but it still wasn't too late to save herself, to keep herself emotionally intact. She was convinced of that. She had taken control of her own life when she went off to college, and that wasn't about to change now. She wouldn't let it!

She slammed down the lid of the chest, and then lifted it up again to tuck in a wayward corner of the lavender gown. The poor thing shouldn't suffer just because of Cal Bonner.

She headed for her parents' house without quite knowing why, just knowing that she had to go there. She had been badly shaken, and that old house on Lincoln Street still held every breath she had ever taken as a child, when troubles were few, her heart mostly glad, full and free.

Chapter Five

As she turned onto Lincoln, a neat street shaded by mature elm trees, Meredith spotted her mother; she was in fast pursuit of what was either the strangest-looking dog Meredith had ever seen or a small pig.

She pulled over to the curb, stopped the van, and joined in the chase. She wasn't surprised to discover that it was a pig they were chasing across Mrs. Henderson's petunias and through the Nadels' geraniums. She had shared quarters with stranger things while growing up in Roxanne's Animal Ark. That was what her father had affectionately dubbed their house years ago, because of his wife's compulsion for taking in strays. "Somebody has to do it," was Roxanne's motto, which the entire family had to live with, in a sort of revolving-door animal shelter that had included, among other things, a ferret, bobcat, and two or three peacocks.

They managed to corner the pig, which was about the size of Jo Jo the Lhasa, in the Jensons' yard. As they headed for the van, Roxanne carrying the squealing pig, Meredith put an arm around her mother's shoulder and said, "Mom, you're really weird."

"So you're father's been telling me for thirty years," Roxanne said, not quite laughing, but laughing with her eyes. "This is Meredith, by the way," she added, lovingly kissing the pig's smooth, pink head. "I hope you don't mind me naming a pig after you . . . oh, I could just wring Flossie Pembrook's neck. Her daughter—you remember Sheila, don't you? I believe she was in the same grade as you.''

''She's Joleen's age,'' Meredith reminded her. ''Isn't she married to Troy Beckman?''

''Was. They're divorced,'' Roxanne said in a hushed voice, as if she were divulging classified information that might threaten national security. Crystal Creek was thirty miles from Dallas, and about a hundred light-years from life as most people lived it. Here divorce was still spoken about in whispered voices. ''Anyway,'' Roxanne resumed, ''Meredith here belonged to Sheila, and when she and Troy split up she hightailed it over to Dallas. I think she's working for some big fancy law firm. Not that it matters one way or the other. She left this sweet baby with her mother . . . and I know that Flossie is a Christian woman, but she's one of those people who doesn't think animals have feelings. You know the kind. She stuck this baby out in her backyard, tied to a tree! Well, you know me. I pitched three kinds of fits. One thing led to another, and now Meredith belongs to me. I suppose I'll eventually have to take her out to your grandfather's place. But what are we standing around here for in the hot sun? Let's get to the house. I've just made some strudel.''

Meredith stared at her mother. She was a petite woman who didn't look her age; in fact, in her sloppy T-shirt and blue jeans, her shoulder-length red hair swept up in a ponytail, she could have passed for Meredith's sister instead of a forty-seven-year-old grandmother of many. But one thing she had never been was a cook.

''Mother, you don't know how to make strudel,'' Meredith said.

"Of course I don't. I can't boil water without burning it. But I've discovered all sorts of frozen goodies since you gave me and your dad that microwave oven for Christmas last year—and was Flossie ever pea green with envy! All Sheila gave her was a blender."

Sure enough, Roxanne turned out a mean apple strudel, from the frozen food section of Grant's Market and directly to her microwave. Meredith ate hers balancing a kitten on each knee; another climbed around the kitchen table. Five dogs were at various locations in the large room, that, like the gingerbread-trimmed exterior, needed a fresh coat of paint. Somehow all the animals that had lived at Roxanne's Animal Ark at one time or another always got fed, as had the Grant clan, even on a sheriff's salary. At the bottom of the priority list was paint for the house.

Meredith recognized Sam, the Irish setter, Cocoa the Labrador retriever, and Jo Jo the Lhasa. The other two dogs were new additions. A spitz named Happy, and a medium-sized dog with a perpetual wagging tail called Sarge whose breed was in question. The kittens were Faith, Hope, and Charity. Meredith had tripped over two ducks on the way inside the house. Easter gifts neighborhood kids had received, her mother said. And once they'd grown out of the cute stage the ducks had worn out their welcome. Roxanne Grant had shook her head, deploring the state of the world. Fortunately, Meredith's grandfather was more than happy to take in those animals that needed the wide-open spaces of country living, or a pond. Roxanne did her best to place all the animals in "forever homes," but her adoption procedures were grueling, and few passed the exam.

"I'm so happy to see you, dear," Roxanne said as she plunked two cups of mint tea down on the butcher-block table. "I was beginning to think you'd never get around to dropping by for a visit. You're always in such a rush. But I suppose that old house is keeping you plenty busy." She bustled around the table. "Do you remember that dog you loved so much when you were a little girl?"

Meredith grinned. "Teddy. He was as ornery as the day is long, but he was the best friend I've ever had."

Roxanne tore off a piece of the strudel and dropped it so close to the pig that "Meredith" almost ended up wearing it for a hat, before gobbling it up, like a pig. Roxanne scrutinized the human Meredith silently for a moment. *Seriously* scrutinized, then she said, "You look like you could use a friend now. What's wrong, Mere?"

"Nothing." Meredith took a spoonful of sugar and dumped it into her cup. The two kittens that had been on her knees joined their sister on the table, knocking over the sugar bowl as they played a game of chase. Roxanne didn't seem to notice the spilled sugar.

She said, "Honey, you never could bluff your way out of a wet paper sack. Didn't you know that's why your brothers always wanted you to play poker with them? How many times did you lose your baby-sitting money to those scamps?"

"A lot." Meredith stood up and moved restlessly around the kitchen. She had always been able to talk to her mother about anything, but this was a new experience for her, and she didn't know where to begin. "Mom, are you happy?" she said instead.

Roxanne laughed. "Good heavens, where did that come from? Am I happy? I suppose so. Why?"

"I was just wondering if . . . well, if you didn't ever want something more than just being Daddy's wife or our mother?"

"My, you *are* in a mood, aren't you, Mere?" Roxanne

added some of the spilled sugar to her tea and scrutinized her daughter again. "This wouldn't have anything to do with that good-looking young man who bought the House of the Seasons, would it?"

"For pity sakes, Mother, how did you jump to that conclusion?"

"Wishful thinking, maybe. A woman just isn't complete until she finds that one certain man."

"Mother!"

"Just as a man isn't complete until he finds the woman meant for him. Look at your father and me."

Meredith stopped pacing. It was on the tip of her tongue to point out that, as lovable and wonderful as her father was, he still lived in a world of absolutes that began and ended with a woman's place being in the home and the man bringing home the bacon . . . with apologies to Meredith the pig, who was curled up around Roxanne's feet now, sound asleep, as were the kittens on the table, and all the dogs, except for Sarge; he was wagging his tail. Her mother looked sort of cute, and sort of pathetic in this setting. And Meredith couldn't help asking her, "Mom, did you ever regret getting married so young?"

Roxanne laughed again. "When would I have had the time? I had four babies before I knew what was causing them, and by the time Bo came along I was too pooped to pop. That's why I depended on you so much, Mere. Too much, probably. But if you want the truth, I can't imagine my life any other way. I fell in love with your daddy when I was seven, married him when I was seventeen, and I still get goose bumps when I hear his car pull up in the drive."

Meredith went over and kissed Roxanne's cheek. The skin was still fresh and youthful, and smelled comfortingly of Ivory soap. "I have to run, Mom. Say hello to Daddy for me."

"Can't you stay for supper? Joleen and Travis are going to be here with their kids."

"Some other time."

"Very well, but come back soon, Mere, and bring your young man with you."

"Mother, there is no young man."

"Whatever you say, dear, but I'd still like to meet him."

Meredith left the house, shaking her head. At least now she knew why she'd come here today. It wasn't just for maternal comfort. She needed to remind herself what could happen when a woman gave up her independence, her identity, for a man. Her mother was little more than an extension of her father. Maybe that was enough for Roxanne, but Meredith was the butterfly that left the cocoon, and she had stopped following Grant house rules when she was eighteen . . . and she would never let her memories become more important than her dreams!

She had no intentions of pursuing any man, least of all Cal Bonner—especially Cal Bonner! She wasn't foolish enough to believe independence meant automatic happiness, whatever that meant, but she wouldn't let any man take charge of her life.

"That's right, Cal," she declared, climbing back into her van and accelerating forcefully. "Especially not you!"

Chapter Six

The front two-thirds of the newspaper office was a single bay, cut up into individual cubicles by shoulder-high dividers, exactly the kind used in small-town dailies. But since the *Chronicle* was a weekly, the staff was limited to two full-time employees. Jack Murphy, a heavyset man with Coke-bottle glasses, sat in front of an individual monitor, drinking coffee. Ellen Grant, a half-pint ball of energy two months out of her teens, with wispy brown hair that flew off in every direction, was staring at a computer terminal as if confronting an alien from another planet. When Meredith walked in, they both glanced up.

"Mere, what are you doing here?" her cousin asked.

"I need to see your boss. Is he in?"

"Sure, but you don't have an appointment, do you?"

"Do I need one?"

"Naw. I'll just announce you." Ellen giggled. "That's the way Mr. Bonner says things are done in the big city."

"That's okay, Ellen. I'll announce myself." The prospect of venturing into Cal's office was daunting, but Meredith had spent the rest of the weekend searching for a way out of her financial bind, only to return again and again to the same inevitable solution.

She exchanged pleasantries with Jack Murphy, a good

friend of her brother Andy, as she passed by his cubicle. Jack's desk was neat, in contrast with Ellen's, which was a swamp of papers and souvenirs. Three different kinds of gray or putty-colored metal file cabinets were stuck wherever there was space. Old fliers, notes, cartoons, and journalistic missives were tacked or taped on walls and bulletin boards. A brown plastic radio the size of a toaster, the kind last made in the sixties with a big, round tuning dial, sat on top of a file cabinet, a bent steel clothes hanger jammed into the back as an antenna. An adenoidal voice squeaked from the primitive speaker, giving a weather report for a hot, dry day.

Meredith took a deep breath, lifted her head, and sailed into the tiny office at the back of the building.

"Good morning, Cal," she said cheerily. "It's darker than a tomb in here, for crying out loud. There . . . that's better." Meredith yanked on the blinds, sending a dazzle of sunlight into the fluorescent-lit room.

"You do have a way of taking over a room," Cal said dryly. He was standing over an open file cabinet that was identical to the ones in the outer office. Putty-colored. It matched the walls, and was a perfect compliment for the seedy tone of the rest of the room. But that didn't stop him from looking fresh and vibrant, as if he'd just stepped off a tropical beach. Meredith imagined him on a stretch of Maui sand, his hair wind-rumpled above a rakish smile.

Why on earth did he have to affect her like this?

She sank down in a hard-backed chair across from his battered desk, her dress of sapphire blue settling in soft folds about her. Cal's eyes swept over her as he moved around a big, unwieldy chair and settled into it. They had not seen each other since their kiss in the attic, but Meredith's heart still felt bruised. He had rejected her that day; perhaps only a glamorous and sophisticated woman like Cynthia Campbell could touch his heart. Meredith sat up a little straighter, reminding herself fiercely that emotional independence was the most important thing in the world to her. She had to hold on to it.

"What can I do for you?" Cal asked curtly.

Meredith struggled to gaze back at him with equanimity. "You really should do something about this place. It has no personality at all."

The barest trace of a smile crossed his mouth. "Did you come here to decorate my office?"

Her eyes idly raked the room. Everything was 1960s-ish except for the IBM computer on Cal's desk. "That's not a bad idea," she said. "But I wanted to talk to you about your house. It's really coming along well, isn't it?" she asked brightly. He drummed his fingers on the scarred desk. He looked powerful and dynamic, his hair springing back from his forehead in the way she found so appealing.

"Every wall half-painted," he said. "Stacks of tiles in my bathtub. Curtains all over the chairs but none on the windows. You haven't finished one single room. That's not what I call 'coming along well.' "

"I'm glad you brought up that point, Cal. You see, I work with an overall scheme in mind. It's very important to stay in keeping with the entire spirit of the house."

"Why? Is the place haunted? Are you trying to pacify ghosts?"

"My brother Paul says it is, and the House of the Seasons does have a history. We can't ignore that."

"Of course not," he muttered. "We wouldn't want to just paint the thing and be done with it."

She smiled at him. He didn't smile back.

"Meredith, I assume there is a point to all this."

She sighed. He wasn't making things easy for her. It wasn't as though she'd wanted to come here today. She didn't have any other choice, that was all. Poking through her briefcase, she extracted a slightly wrinkled sheet of paper. She pushed it across the desk. "I wanted you to see exactly what I've spent so far. I wanted you to have the whole picture."

He scowled down at the paper. "Are you serious? It takes that many cans of paint to come up with persimmon pink? I hate pink."

"I'm using it very judiciously—as an accent color."

"Why did you buy me a wok? And I don't need a Gothic arch mirror."

"Yes, you do. It's going to look wonderful in the dining room. It's European country, with marvelous embossed detailing on its frame. I can hardly wait to get it up."

Cal did not seem to share her enthusiasm. "What's this about more carpentry work?" he demanded. "You told me you were only going to have a few repairs done."

"I know you'll be happy with the extra shelf space that's being put in, and closets. And I think one of the carpenters has a crush on Kayanne. His name is Tony, and he's very enterprising." Meredith saw from the expression on Cal's face that this information wasn't going over too well. In fact, the entire discussion wasn't proceeding as planned. She had wanted to prove to Cal that she knew exactly where his money had gone, and that each expenditure was completely justified. Somehow she didn't seem to be getting this across to him. She decided to plunge right ahead.

"You see, Cal, the house has required a greater initial

outlay than I anticipated. I'll therefore have to request an additional amount of money from you.'' She pushed another sheet of paper toward him, this one smudged from a great deal of figuring, erasing, and more figuring. ''You can see it all right there. I'll need to purchase more furnishings, of course, and settle up with the carpenters. By the way, I'm sure you'll agree that I'm being very reasonable about the fee for all my extra time.'' She felt triumphant now that the words were out, although Cal's expression still wasn't encouraging.

''You signed an agreement, Meredith. I'm not obligated to hand over one more cent to you until the job is finished.''

''Things have evolved since then,'' she protested.

''Is this how you usually operate your business?'' he asked in a quiet but steely tone. ''Your renege on agreements and buy woks for people who don't want them?''

''The House of the Seasons is a special case. It's been neglected, for a long time. Besides, there is a difference between the letter of the law and the spirit of it—''

''Spirits again! Let's stick with facts here,'' he interrupted. ''For one thing, who does your books?''

''I handle my own accounting, with Kayanne's help. She's very good with numbers.''

Cal rubbed his jaw. ''What was your net profit last year?''

''Net profit?'' Meredith shifted in her chair. ''Um . . . it wasn't bad.''

''You're not really sure, are you? You probably took a loss.''

''Not much of one,'' she said defensively. ''And I don't see that it's any of your business, anyway.''

Ignoring the remark, Cal went on in that calm, relentless tone. "What kind of advertising campaign do you have?"

"We're in the Yellow Pages," she said proudly. "Grant Designs. You can look it up. This wouldn't be a pitch for me to buy space in the *Chronicle,* would it?"

"I doubt that you could afford it. Do you know what deductions to make on your tax return? Do you depreciate your business equipment? Have you established a good, solid relationship with your banker? Do you even *have* a banker?"

"That's none of your business," she muttered.

Cal raised an eyebrow. "It's worse than I thought. You run your business like a one-woman demolition derby. For your own good, I'm not going to give you any more money."

Meredith was not defeated. She stood up so that she could give Cal her most forceful glare. For added emphasis, she leaned across his desk. "We're talking about your house, Cal. Your home! It could be a real home, too, if you'd just let me do my job. The kind of place that has a stack of firewood by the hearth and wind chimes on the veranda." Meredith's cheeks were flushed, the blood pumping through her body. She forgot all the arguments she'd rehearsed in front of her mirror, and the words just tumbled out of her. She looked straight into Cal's eyes.

"I know you better than you think I do, Cal Bonner. And I know that what you want deep down is a place to remind you of that drafty old farmhouse in France that has such wonderful memories for you. A place far removed from Highland Park mansions and country estates. But you want a place that's different, too. Your own personal idea of what a home should be. The House of the Seasons is what you've been searching for, even if you don't know it yet. You've seen it—the home that could be. I see it, too. That's why you can't turn me down, Cal. It's *your* vision of the house I'm bringing to life!''

She stopped, out of breath and rather alarmed by what she'd said. She hadn't realized any of this before today, but every instinct told her it was the truth; she and Cal shared the same dream of what a home should be. The dream bound them together with its power, perhaps irrevocably. Her arms were trembling as she pressed her hands against Cal's desk. He gazed at her seriously, all mockery gone.

Neither of them said anything for a long moment. Then Cal brought out a checkbook and started writing in it, his pen scratching over the paper. Meredith straightened, drained by the encouter. Cal tore off the check and handed it to her.

''Thank you,'' she said formally, depositing it in her briefcase.

''None of this changes my mind, Meredith. You've still gone too far with my house. *Way* too far. And you definitely need help managing your business.''

''I'm happy with things the way they are.''

''A manager would help you channel your money and time. You'd be more productive.''

''I'm already productive. And right now I don't have to answer to anyone else. I'm going to keep it that way.''

''You're making a mistake.''

She ignored his warning, glancing around at his putty-colored walls and sixties-ish furniture. ''You really should let me do something with this office.''

''I'll think about it,'' he said agreeably. ''Maybe we should do it in persimmon pink.''

She frowned at him. He looked far too attractive with his devilish grin.

"Good-bye, Cal." She swept out of the room and past Jack and Ellen, both grinning sheepishly; they had obviously overheard the exchange. *Well, I don't need anybody telling me how to manage my business,* Meredith thought. Everything was under control: the carpenters would get their money, Kayanne and Bo would have a few weeks' salary, and she could pay her electric bill.

Most important of all, she would continue furnishing Cal's house like a real home.

Over the next few days Meredith lavished her love on the old place, bringing all sorts of gifts to it—an antique rolltop desk, an authentic butter churn, two large bath towels decorated with black Scotties in red bows. It was like celebrating the home's long-forgotten birthdays.

By the time Saturday came around again, Meredith had also purchased the tools needed to make her advance into the garden. She spent a contented morning raking up ancient leaves and poking into hardened earth with a spade. Then she crawled under the hedge, humming to herself and enjoying the good, clean snap of shears on dead branches.

She heard the sound of a car driving up, and a moment later an elegant pair of high-heeled shoes strolled into her line of vision. The shoes were glossy red patent leather, cut in simple lines to display a graceful set of ankles. Meredith inched herself out from under the hedge and stood up. Cynthia Campbell faced her, looking polished in a white linen suit and red silk blouse. Meredith glanced down at her own T-shirt with its ripped hem and her denim shorts, which were cutoffs from a pair of worn-out old jeans. Just being around Cynthia Campbell made her feel inadequate. Cynthia's assurance was obviously more than skin-deep; she carried herself like a woman who had believed in herself since babyhood. Yet she was not dismissive today, and she greeted Meredith pleasantly.

"Hello there," she said. "I was looking for Cal, but I suppose he isn't home."

"No, he's not," Meredith answered.

"That's too bad. I wanted to ask him to pick me up early before the tasting tonight."

"Tasting?"

"Wine tasting," Cynthia clarified. "It's a preview of the new 1989 Veuve Clicquot and four others—a decade of Vintage Reserve, as it were. Hosted by Frederic Panaiotis at the Crescent Court's Beau Nash Restaurant. Mr. Panaiotis is an oenologist at the Maison Clicquot estate in Reims, France."

Meredith nodded, as if what Cynthia had just said made sense. It didn't, and it hurt far too much to know that Cal was going out with Cynthia again. "I'm sure you can call him later," Meredith said mechanically.

"Yes, I'll do that," Cynthia said, but she made no move to leave. Instead, she perched herself on the edge of the marble fountain, her beautiful long legs crossed casually at the ankles. "Cal was telling me how you're transforming his house," she went on. "He says you're quite a talented decorator."

Meredith was skeptical about that last comment. The Cal she knew was less than flattering of what she'd been doing to his house. She smiled a little to herself.

"I'm sure it's a very gratifying experience, working with Cal," Cynthia said. "Just between us girls, Meredith, he's quite an unusual man."

"I suppose you could say that," Meredith answered cautiously, unsure where this conversation was headed.

"It's not just that he's so attractive, although that certainly counts for a lot," Cynthia elaborated. "He's intelligent, sensitive, and caring. He also has the potential to be one of the most successful advertising executives in the country. Even his father recognizes that."

Meredith picked a twig out of her hair. Yes, Cal Bonner was all those things, as well as pigheaded, impatient, and opinionated. He wouldn't be nearly as interesting a person without such traits. Cynthia almost made him sound like a saint. How dull that would be!

Cynthia was observing her too carefully, Meredith thought, annoyed by the undercurrents she sensed.

"How much of your message do you actually want me to relay to Cal?" she asked without ceremony.

"Oh, Cal already knows what high regard I have for him," Cynthia said easily. "We go back a long way, Cal and I. I was just wondering how you felt about him, Meredith, and it's obvious that you share my opinion."

Meredith said nothing to this, sure that Cynthia would use any information she gleaned today to suit her own purposes. At last Cynthia stood up, shaking back her lustrous mane of hair. Her eyes were impossible to read.

"I've enjoyed chatting with you, Meredith," she said, sounding companionable and completely sincere. "I'd like to talk to you again sometime. I might be able to throw some decorating business your way."

"I have more than I can handle right now."

"You should always cultivate your contacts," Cynthia answered coolly. "I could be of invaluable assistance to you in your career. Good-bye now. Please do tell Cal that I stopped by to see him."

Meredith nodded grudgingly, still feeling at a disadvantage. She watched as the silver BMW purred out of the drive and down Fillmore Street.

Cynthia Campbell was an enigma. She had seemed genuinely pleased to talk to Meredith and hadn't sounded patronizing, even when she gave the advice about cultivating contacts. Yet something rang false; Cynthia seemed to have an ulterior motive in coming here today. She probably hadn't intended to see Cal at all. More than likely she'd come to check out the competition.

Meredith poked her fingers into her new pair of flowered gardening gloves. Competing with Cynthia for Cal's affections seemed so foolish, so hazardous. Already she was too bound to Cal, wondering if she would ever be able to break completely free of him. Already she felt too much pain just knowing Cal and Cynthia would spend another evening together.

She pulled off her gloves and tossed them down like gauntlets, in a challenge to herself. She wouldn't succumb to the hurt inside her; she'd battle it with wholesome physical labor.

She strode over to the new lawn mower she'd purchased, and pushed it around to the back of the house where the lawn sloped down before her in a wild tangle of grass. She yanked on the starter and the machine leapt to life, traveling forward with a momentum all its own. Meredith pulled on the handle, but it was already too late. The lawn mower had gained speed and was racing down the steep incline. All she could do was hang on and fly along after it.

They both landed in a clump of tall Johnson grass, and the engine cut off abruptly. Meredith struggled to her feet, brushing off her shorts and craning her neck to stare up at the house. The steepness of the lawn was more than she'd bargained for. But she was not defeated yet. She grasped the handle of the lawn mower and started pulling it back up the hill. Every muscle strained against the forces of gravity. She advanced a little, then a little more.

"What's going on now?" Cal's voice demanded from above her. She stopped, sweat trickling down her face. She didn't dare look up for fear of losing her grip.

"Hi, Cal. I'm mowing, as you can see."

"I can see, all right."

"If you don't mind, I'll just get on with it." Meredith licked the corner of her mouth. Her hands were beginning to slip from perspiration and she bent back a little further against the weight of the machine.

"You're supposed to be an interior decorator," Cal's voice shot down at her. "Not an exterior one!"

"Well, you know what we were talking about the other day," she panted. "My overall scheme? If I'm going to look at the house—as a whole—I have to include the lawn—" The mower slipped out of her grasp and went crashing down the hill. She tried to look as if that was exactly what she'd intended. Taking out her handkerchief—Cal's handkerchief that she could never remember to return to him—she patted her face.

Cal climbed down beside her. He seemed ready for a good argument. But then he simply looked at her; his gaze felt like a caress.

"Sunlight," he said musingly. "You have eyes full of sunlight. Did you know that?"

Meredith stared at the soft cotton of his shirt. She stood without moving, almost without breathing. She knew she should turn away from him before her defenses crumbled. Yet everything in her ached to be near him.

"Cynthia came by," she blurted out, using the words as a barrier. "She wanted you to pick her up early tonight . . . before the wine tasting."

Cal looked puzzled. "What wine tasting? Nobody told me about this."

"I'd be happy to, except I didn't understand a word she said. Something about some French guy and a decade of something or the other."

Cal groaned. "Cynthia keeps arranging these evenings of hers without consulting me first. I hate wine."

Meredith rubbed a scrape on her elbow, feeling a surge of relief and happiness. So the evening entertainment was all Cynthia's idea, not Cal's. The intensity of her emotions startled her, although it shouldn't have. Anything to do with Cal Bonner seemed to affect her this way—no half-measures allowed. He reached out a hand and gently cupped her chin. Now a sensual lassitude took her over, as if his touch could still all her fears of him. Her lips parted and her breath came on a slow, deep sigh.

"We seem to have a problem," she managed to say. "This physical attraction—both of us . . ."

"We ought to be able to work it out," Cal said. "We're two adults."

"Two responsible adults," she agreed. She curled her fingers to keep them from reaching out to him.

"So we won't take this any further," he said.

"We did agree to be professional." She raised her eyes slowly to his.

"Yeah, right." He bent his head and kissed her, his lips firm and demanding. She returned the kiss steadily, making her own demands.

Then it was over. Cal lifted his head and stepped back from her. "There," he said.

She widened her eyes. "Well. Now that that's out of the way—" she began.

"Don't you feel better?"

She wouldn't admit it, but she did feel better. This time there was no horrible sense of rejection, no coldness afterward. It had been a most satisfying kiss, exquisitely complete in itself. How could Cal's lips tutor her in so many different emotions?

She made herself speak in a calm, analytical manner. "We're going to ruin our business relationship," she said. "If we keep on this way we won't be able to avoid it."

"We can't deny the attraction between us," he said, sounding equally reasonable. "That's what we've been trying to do and it's not working. Maybe we're more than business associates. Have you thought about that?"

"We're not exactly friends, though," she said quickly. "We're more than acquaintances, of course, but I really do think associates is the right term to describe us." She stopped, chagrined to find that Cal was regarding her with open amusement.

"You have to put a label on it, don't you?" he asked. "You have to make sure all the limits are strictly defined so I don't get too close to you."

"We both agreed on those limits," she said shakily. "We both agreed it would be a professional relationship, nothing more."

"Why are you so afraid of me, Meredith?" His voice was gentle. "I don't want to hurt you. I just want us to be honest with each other." He reached out a hand to her but she backed away, folding her arms against her body.

"All right, let's be really honest," she said, challenge in her voice. "Where do you see our relationship heading?"

"I don't know," he said slowly. "That's the whole

point, isn't it? There aren't any signposts along the way to tell us where we're going.''

''So you don't want to set any limits?'' Meredith scoffed. ''That's the best escape because it means you don't have to commit yourself to anything.''

''You're the one who's frightened, Meredith. You behave as if any minute prison bars are going to come slamming down in front of your face. It shows in everything you do—the way you run your business.''

''You're not going to start that again.'' Meredith moved down the sloping yard and grasped the handle of the lawn mower. Cal followed her.

''We have to talk about it,'' he said ominously. ''I found your note asking for more money taped to the refrigerator. That was a nice touch.''

''I wanted to make sure you saw it as soon as possible.''

''I suppose you thought it would be easy to ask me for more money because you succeeded so well the first time. You want my help with no strings attached. It's another symptom of your fear that you'll lose control of your life.''

''I've had enough psychoanalysis for one day, though it is very enlightening. Thank you for explaining to me that independence in a woman is something abnormal and neurotic.''

''You're deliberately misinterpreting what I say. Cynthia Campbell is an independent woman, and I admire that in her. She knows how to use her independence.''

This was too much. Meredith started pulling on the mower. She was angry, but most of all she felt wounded. Cal had compared her to Cynthia and found her lacking. She didn't seemed to have any defense against that; it hit her too deep and too hard. *Oh, blast!* Couldn't Cal see that she just wanted him to leave her alone? But he wouldn't give it up.

"Wait a minute," he said. "You're a danger to yourself." He took over the lawn mower and hauled it up the hill. She had no choice other than to scramble up alongside. At the top, he stopped and surveyed the jagged strip of mown grass that marked her earlier descent. To his credit, Cal maintained a solemn expression.

"I think we'd better try another system," he said. She couldn't argue, although she would have liked to. Cal disappeared into the shed, which had scallops of trim that matched the house. He emerged with some rope after a moment. Rolling up his sleeves, he squatted down next to the mower. Meredith watched the deft movements of his hands. He tied the rope at the base of the handle, then stood up again.

"All right, I'm going to be holding on to the rope to keep the mower steady for you. Move in rows across the lawn, not down. Definitely not down. Got that?"

"Yes, sir," she said acidly. He glanced at her.

"Good, let's go." He pulled the starter. Fortunately, the engine had survived its tumbles and started right up.

Meredith had to admit that Cal had devised a good plan. He walked with her as she mowed, using his rope to work against the machine's weight on the steep incline. She was free to make satisfying, even rows in the shaggy grass. And she was free to wonder what other comparisons Cal had made between Cynthia and herself. Would Meredith always come up on the short end of the stick?

"I can't believe you need more money already," Cal shouted over the roar of the engine. Meredith turned and started another row. He moved along with her.

"The house is crying out for attention," she declared loudly.

"There's a new Tiffany lamp in the library."

"I know. Isn't it wonderful?"

"And a circus wagon on the mantel."

"It's an antique. Did you see the workmanship?"

"Those aren't exactly necessities, Meredith."

"I disagree." She plowed on ahead, but Cal kept right with her at the end of that stupid rope.

"This is a lot more serious than I thought at first," he yelled over the engine. Meredith mowed furiously.

"You hired me to do a job, Cal," she yelled back. "That's what I'm doing."

"Your business is in trouble, Meredith. You have to face that."

She turned to retort, but then slipped and had to cling to the mower to keep from falling. The only thing holding both of them upright was Cal, straining at the other end of the rope.

Meredith regained her balance. She reached over, shut off the engine, then plunked herself down in the grass. Cal took hold of the lawn mower.

"This is an expensive one," he said. His voice reverberated in the sudden stillness. Meredith mopped her face with his handkerchief.

"It's also a good one," she said. "It will last you a very long time. Quality counts."

"You assistant called me at the newspaper today, asking if I'd seen you. She said she'd been trying to reach you all morning. She sounded almost incoherent."

Meredith looked warily at him over the handkerchief. "Kayanne? She's not just my assistant, she's my baby sister. I'll call her right back. I'm sure it's nothing. I was

... um, out in the garden for a while and couldn't hear the telephone.''

"She kept talking about little tables and big cushions. And a Mrs. Lidcome, who wants her money back right away.''

"Lipscomb,'' Meredith muttered.

"What?''

"Mrs. Lipscomb. That's who Kayanne is talking about. I apologize for my sister. She shouldn't be going on like that to you. It's an inconvenience—''

"She sounded pretty upset, Meredith. I think she has good reason to be.''

Meredith stuffed the handkerchief back into her pocket. "I can handle my own business affairs,'' she said tightly.

Cal leaned against the mower. "I don't think you can.''

She stared at him. "I've had enough of this. First you come out here and kiss me. Then you tie a rope to my lawn mower ... *your* lawn mower—''

"You needed kissing.''

Meredith struggled to her feet. "I don't need anything from you, Cal Bonner!''

He took a slip of paper out of his pocket and examined it. "Another request for money, with sunflowers painted all over it.''

"Just tear it up. I'll do without it.''

He gazed at her speculatively. "I think you do need this money, Meredith. Rather badly, too.''

"Not anymore.'' She searched her mind frantically. There had to be other options.

"I'll give you a check right now,'' Cal went on imperturbably. "All the money you need to finish the job. On one condition.''

"I really don't want to hear this—"

"The condition is that you let me do some financial planning for you."

She brushed loose grass away from herself with determination. "If you're such a financial genius, why did your father ship you off to the boondocks instead of keeping you at the corporate office?"

"He has a warped sense of humor."

"The apple doesn't fall far from the tree, does it? But I have a policy, Cal. No one looks at my checkbook except me."

"Afraid of what they'll find?"

She sighed. "Look, I have a father, too, and I love him dearly. But he doesn't allow my mother any power at all. So she takes the checkbook when he's not looking and she writes checks without recording them. You can get away with an overdrawn account in a small town. The bank just sits on it until the next deposit. It's confusing, but it seems to work. Anyway, my mother spends money like it's going out of style on her animals. Once she even pawned her wedding ring to pay for medicine some of her dogs needed. She won't admit it but I always believed it's a subtle rebellion."

Cal started chuckling.

Meredith glared at him. "It's not funny! That's pathetic! I don't have to sneak around trying to filch money from someone else. So there's no reason anybody has to look into my finances."

Cal straightend and shrugged. "Those are my terms, and I suspect you don't have anywhere else to turn. Just think of it, Meredith. I'll supply you with enough money to buy anything and everything you want for the house, along with a generous amount to cover your time. How can you refuse a deal like that?"

She clenched her hands. Oh, the look of satisfaction on his face. He knew he had her, all right. The house needed everything she could give it; that was why she was in this fix. She'd always been able to get by before, no matter how precarious the situation.

But she wouldn't blame the house. Cal was enjoying his power over her. She knew he was, even though his face was impassive. He could dominate her senses with one touch, one kiss. That didn't seem to be enough for him, though. He wanted to take over the rest of her while keeping his own self intact.

She tilted her chin. ''Okay, Cal. You win—for now.''

Chapter Seven

"I hate rich people," Meredith muttered. She let her irritation show.

But Cal put up a warning hand. "We have an agreement, Meredith, remember?"

"How could I possibly forget?" Cal had lost no time in consolidating his victory. He had been waiting when she arrived at his house early on this Monday morning, and the next thing she knew he was dragging her back to Dallas. He wouldn't explain what he was up to, but pulled his Jaguar into a Turtle Creek parking lot, then escorted her firmly to a building Meredith thought had been designed by a seriously snobby architect: black windows, aluminum triangles, and copper flashing, snuggled into the lush foliage and parklike setting of the historic and fashionable winding creek area. The building was directly across from the world-renowned five-star hotel and restaurant The Mansion.

New Dimensions, that was the name on the snobby building. Meredith didn't like the sound of it. She stopped in her tracks and resisted as Cal took her by the elbow.

"Meredith, we can't stand here all day," he said.

"I'm moving," she grumbled.

"You couldn't prove it by me."

"This is a mistake—I won't let you do this to me!"

But today Cal was taking full advantage of his financial hold over her.

"You don't have any choice." His eyes were as implacable as stone. *Blast the man!* He was behaving as if he owned her, body and soul. She already had enough complications in her life; for one thing, Mrs. Lipscomb was becoming more intractable every day. Not only did the woman refuse to pay what she owed on her account, now she wanted all her money refunded and every trace of the French antiques eradicated immediately—if not sooner—from her house. Meredith and Kayanne had managed to establish only a precarious truce with Mrs. Lipscomb. Meredith was on edge, and Cal commandeering her like this didn't help.

He prodded her across a bridge over a cattail-ringed pond. A cluster of ducks rooted through the shallow water weeds for the kernels of corn somebody had thrown into the water. Strips of sunshine, broken by the green branches of weeping willows, dappled the pond. The parking lot around them was sprinkled with luxury cars: BMW, Mercedes, Lexus, Cadillac, and Cal's Jaguar.

"Speaking of rich," Meredith said.

"Behave yourself," Cal said, and opened the gleaming doors of New Dimensions. Her feet sank into lush, deep wine carpet as she brushed past an arty rectangle decorated with a blue bird and a hanging bird cage enclosing a talking mynah. The walls had a slight pinkish tinge; all the pictures on them were of birds.

"What's with all the birds?" Meredith asked with contempt. "What kind of place is this?"

Cal ushered her into the elevator. The doors shut silently behind them, and they were completely enclosed in a box of painted flamingos.

"I don't believe this," Meredith said. Cal leaned against the wall next to her.

"Why don't you just relax and enjoy the ride?" he asked with a lazy grin. "You look like a prisoner about to walk the last mile."

"That's exactly how I feel."

Cal's hand gently clasped her elbow again. "Trust me, Meredith," he murmured. "This isn't going to be so bad."

She gazed at his three-button checked sportcoat, unable to pull away from him. Her heartbeat had quickened at his nearness, and she breathed in the subtle pine scent of his after-shave. She needed all her defenses right now, and yet she just wanted to go on standing close to Cal.

The elevator glided to a smooth halt.

"Any last words before you're strapped into the chair?" he asked. Meredith sent him a venomous glance, which seemed to have no effect at all. The doors slid open, and he propelled her into a hall painted with more birds.

Cynthia Campbell was waiting there, very sleek in a black-and-white jacket dress that showed to full advantage her long, shapely legs. Meredith stared at her, perplexed and dismayed. She had not expected to see Cynthia today, and she turned to Cal for an explanation. He offered none, gazing back at her unperturbed. It was Cynthia who took over.

"Meredith, I'm so glad you could meet with Cal and me," she said in her distinctive, throaty voice. "In a moment we'll explain everything to you. What a lovely jacket you're wearing." She smiled appreciatively at Meredith's yellow silk blazer, then led the way down the hall. Cal went on holding Meredith to his side as they followed Cynthia into a large, elegant office furnished in contemporary cherry furniture. Birds leapt out from prints along the walls. The city of Dallas unfolded outside the thirteenth-floor windows, with an eye-popping view of uptown.

Cynthia swung into a chair behind a massive desk, her long, silky hair flowing, her flawless skin unmarred by even one freckle. A disturbing emotion filtered to the surface of Meredith's consciousness—envy. She was envious of Cynthia Campbell! Automatically she sat down beside Cal in one of three leather chairs facing Cynthia's desk, appalled that she could be feeling this way.

"Meredith, I've explained to Cynthia that I'm your financial adviser," Cal was saying. She winced at his words. Financial adviser—he might as well be her jailer! She looked back at him coolly, briefcase propped up in her lap.

Cynthia demanded her attention again. "Yes, Meredith, Cal and I have discussed some exciting options for your future. We believe that the first step is to introduce you to New Dimensions." She reached across the desk and handed Meredith a booklet that had a flamingo on the cover. "This is a profile of New Dimensions that you'll find very interesting," she said with conviction. "Go ahead—you can look through it right now. You'll see that New Dimensions is a large, solvent firm. We develope real estate and we operate everything from shopping malls to luxury hotels."

Meredith didn't understand why Cynthia was delivering this sales pitch. She flipped through the booklet and saw columns of revenue figures, photographs of New Dimensions employees smiling widely into the camera, a picture of a Houston hotel, another in Bel-Air and New Orleans, an artist's rendition of another hotel soon to rise in San Francisco, a thirteen-acre shopping mall under construction in Denver. None of it meant a thing to Meredith. She snapped the booklet shut and placed it back on the desk.

"It's all very exciting, isn't it?" Cynthia asked. She seemed full of lighthearted energy and purpose, as if she were brimming with a delightful secret she couldn't wait to share. Her eyes sparkled. "Cal and I both feel that your company has a great deal of potentinal, Meredith. With the right management it could become enormously successful. New Dimensions can provide that management, leaving you free for the creative end of the business. That's why we asked you here today—to discuss acquiring Grant Designs."

"Acquire?" Meredith echoed faintly. "Cal, what—"

"Just hear us out," he urged, and Cynthia gave her a reassuring smile. The smile didn't convince Meredith at all; she used a similar one herself on clients and suppliers who were being uncooperative.

"I know this probably isn't something you've thought about before," Cynthia said. "Selling your business certainly isn't anything to take lightly. All Cal and I are asking is that you give the idea your consideration." Her low, soothing voice was so persuasive. And the way she kept saying "Cal and I" made the two of them sound like a cozy team working together for the sole benefit of Grant Designs. Cal was talking that way, too.

"We've discussed this at great lengths," Cal said. "Cynthia has been with New Dimensions for several years and has revitalized a number of small businesses. I think it's a good opportunity for you, Meredith."

What Meredith really wanted was an opportunity to slug Cal. She gripped her hands together on top of her briefcase.

"Cal is right. New Dimensions has a great deal to

offer if you come on board with us," Cynthia went on in her low, seductive voice. "Financial security, prestige, unlimited contacts, all the right doors opening up. You'd be decorating the most exclusive homes in the metroplex. You see, New Dimensions can give you power . . . as much as you're willing to reach out and take."

Meredith listened in a daze to this hypnotic recitation. The last words hung dramatically in the air, enticing her. She wondered for a moment what it would be like to have power, and to wield it as confidently as Cynthia Campbell. But thinking of that was like trying on a pair of shoes that didn't fit. Meredith didn't want power— only freedom.

"I'm happy with Grant Designs just the way it is," she asserted, glancing at Cal's impassive face.

"Of course you are," Cynthia agreed. "But think for a moment about the possibility of 'New Dimensions Designs.' Think about all it could mean. You'd go farther than you ever imagined you could." Cynthia took out a sheet of stationery and ran a scarlet fingernail along the top of it. "Just picture the words, right here. 'New Dimensions Designs.' "

Meredith examined the logo: a red sun rising over a flock of flamingos. She could not imagine using this stationery instead of her own flower-embossed notepads. Every month she bought a different design; sometimes she was in the mood for violets, sometimes for a riot of sunflowers. But she would never be in the mood for flamingos!

She glanced up and found Cynthia observing her closely. Cynthia seemed very determined to convince her about all this, and yet surely New Dimensions didn't need a small company like Meredith's. What exactly was going on here? Cynthia Campbell was like a snowflake;

no two facets of her personality were alike. It was impossible to know which facet was the real Cynthia, and what her true motives were.

"I'm going to keep my business," Meredith said steadily. "I've built something under the name Grant Designs. Something that speaks for itself. I'm proud of that and I don't want to lose it."

"I wouldn't expect you to feel any other way," Cynthia answered smoothly. "And we'd want you to go on feeling that way. You see, New Dimensions is a name that can more than speak for itself. You'd have every reason to continue being proud."

Meredith started to argue, but Cal jumped in. "Meredith might feel better about going with New Dimensions if she knew she could retain her present business location," he said.

"Yes, I know we've discussed that, Cal, but I'm not quite clear on a few details." Cynthia gave him a lingering smile before turning back to Meredith. Now she was brisk. "Let me see if I understand this correctly. Exactly what is your business location?"

"Farmer's Branch. That's where I live and work. I save an enormous amount on overhead, and—"

"You run your business from your home?" Cynthia made it sound as if Meredith were fencing stolen goods from her house.

"My business is downstairs. I live upstairs. It's very efficient. Besides, most of my work is done in other people's homes." Meredith's tone was belligerent, and Cynthia seemed to realize she'd gone too far. She switched into her soothing mode again.

"It does sound like a workable system as things stand now. You've been wise to keep your overhead low. But if you join New Dimensions you'll have your headquarters right here in this building. A fashionable address to impress your clients. Come along. I'll show you what kind of office you'd have. I'm sure you'll be absolutely delighted with it.''

She ushered Cal and Meredith out into the hall again and pushed open the door to a large, windowless room.

Meredith closed her eyes and opened them again a second later. The scenery hadn't changed. She saw plush pink carpet, Scandinavian furnishings, and flamingo wall murals on all four sides. Two chairs were upholstered in pink and white stripes. Meredith felt the walls closing in on her, and had a flashback to an old Alfred Hitchcock movie she'd recently seen on television: *The Birds.*

"Isn't it marvelous?" Cynthia asked.

Meredith couldn't speak; she was having enough trouble breathing. She struggled against the wave of claustrophobia that swept over her, determined not to show any weakness in front of Cynthia Campbell. But she couldn't seem to get enough air to breathe. She turned blindly toward Cal, and his hand steadied her arm.

"Meredith and I have another appointment now, Cynthia," she heard him say, his voice sounding very faint. "We have to be going, but we'll meet with you to discuss this again."

"Of course. You look rather ill, Meredith." Cynthia's voice also came from a distance. She sounded solicitous, or perhaps she was only worried that Meredith would be sick in this immaculate office. This immaculate pink office! Meredith swayed a little, determined to keep her stomach under control at all costs.

"We really are late for our appointment," Cal said, his hand still supporting Meredith. "You'll have to excuse us."

"I'll talk to you soon, Cal. . . ."

Meredith didn't feel like herself again until she was outside, away from Cynthia and propped up against the low wall that surrounded New Dimensions. She took several deep breaths of the fresh, pure air.

"I thought you were going to faint right in my arms," Cal said with a concerned look. "Are you all right?"

She nodded shakily. "It was an attack of pink-flamingo phobia, that's all," she said. One of Cal's arms encircled her with its comforting warmth and she had to resist an urge to burrow against him. She stepped back so she could face him squarely. "I'm grateful for the rescue, but how could you do that to me in the first place?" she asked indignantly. "Springing Cynthia Campbell on me!"

Cal rested an elbow on top of the wall. "Would you have agreed to meet with her if I'd told you?"

"Sure—when donkeys fly!"

"That's what I figured, so I had to be underhanded. I know you took an irrational dislike to Cynthia from the moment you met her. Without a little push from me, you wouldn't be able to see what New Dimensions can do for you."

"My dislike for Cynthia is completely rational," Meredith began, then stopped herself when she realized how ridiculous this argument could become. "I don't trust Cynthia, that's all," she said. "And I can't forgive the fact that you discussed Grant Designs with her behind my back. You act as if it's yours to sell!"

"Actually, it was Cynthia who first suggested that New Dimensions might be interested in acquiring you. She's been curious about you ever since I told her you were decorating my house."

"I'll just bet she has," Meredith muttered. "She's up to something and I'd like to know what it is."

"You're being paranoid," Cal said.

"Paranoid? For crying out loud, Cal, surely you can see it, too!" she cried in exasperation. "Cynthia doesn't want me at New Dimensions, and at the same time she does want me there—badly. I'm sure it all has something to do with you, but that's all I'm sure of."

"Cynthia's a businesswoman," Cal pointed out calmly. "There's only one reason she'd make a decision like this—because it would benefit New Dimensions."

Meredith frowned at him, pressing a hand against her damp forehead. "I'm still trying to figure out exactly what Cynthia does," she said. "So far as I can see all she does is snap up little companies and feed them to New Dimensions."

Cal almost smiled. "She doesn't abandon a company once it's acquired. She makes sure the transition goes smoothly for everyone, and she stays in charge of all the management decisions. Cynthia's very good at what she does."

"Obviously *you* think so." Meredith was stung by the way Cal admired Cynthia and defended her. His voice was always emotionless when he spoke of the woman, but he portrayed her as a paragon of the business world. Then another thought struck Meredith, horrible in its implications. "Cal, do you realize what you're asking me to do? You're asking me to let Cynthia Campbell be my boss! I'd go crazy having her order me around."

Cal merely shrugged. "If you'd stop overreacting, you'd see how much New Dimensions could do for your career. Your financial worries would be taken care of, for one thing, and you'd still have a lot of freedom." He gave her a real smile now. A two-hundred-watter. "In fact, your first job for New Dimensions could be to redecorate your new office."

"Oh, sure. Like Cynthia would go for that."

"I think you're judging her too harshly."

"She no doubt has her good points. She *is* stunning."

"What does that have to do with anything?"

"I don't know." Meredith sighed. She wished contrarily that Cal would say Cynthia looked like road kill. There was no chance of that. "I just don't want to lose my independence," she went on more forcefully. "I kept my part of the bargain. You said financial planning, and I've gone this far. That's enough."

"We're only getting started, Meredith." He straightened his shoulders, a forbidding glint in his eyes.

"I won't let you keep manipulating me," she said.

"I'm trying to help you."

"I don't want your help. Or Cynthia's."

"I'm going to hold you to our agreement, whether you like it or not."

She blew her breath out sharply. "I thought no matter what your other faults, at least you were fair-minded."

"What other faults?" he asked. She turned and began striding away.

"Wait a minute. Where are you going?" Cal demanded, easily keeping pace with her.

"To work on the house."

"We came in my car, remember?"

"I'll call Kayanne to pick me up."

"Just stop, will you? I'm not letting you go anywhere. You nearly fainted up there."

"Big deal. I'm fine now. Go find someone else to manage!" She walked faster.

"Stop," he said quietly, taking hold of her arm. "I told Cynthia we had another appointment. You don't want to turn me into a liar, do you?"

"We don't have an appointment, so you've already sinned."

"Wrong. We're going to lunch. I know a nice restaurant over on McKinney Street, not far from here."

Meredith stopped. Deep down she wanted to be with him. She did want to prolong their time together, no matter what. "I know a better one in Fort Worth, a long way from here in Sundance Square, but the Cajun food is worth the drive."

"Sounds great," he said. "I've never been to Sundance Square before."

Meredith was stirred out of that hateful submissiveness. She looked at him in surprise. "I don't believe what I'm hearing. A serious party animal like yourself hasn't hit that lively night spot?"

"Meredith, I'm not like that," he said defensively. "I thought we'd established that fact. I just—"

"I know. You're just a poor misunderstood rich boy who wrecks company cars for a hobby and collects speeding tickets. Well, come on, poor little rich boy. You're in for a real treat."

Whatever visitors to Sundance Square might be in the mood for, they could find it in the downtown region of Fort Worth. Sundance Square was an entertainment and cultural district that was strictly commercial by day, and at night office attire was replaced by party attire, and tennis shoes were traded for dancing shoes.

Meredith led the way through the bustling streets, where Christmas-like decorations were up year-round. There were a variety of new shops and restaurants, and Fire Station Number One, which featured one hundred and fifty years of Fort Worth history. The early 1900s station-turned-museum took visitors back to Fort

Worth's early days. Around the corner from the Conventions and Vistors Bureau was the Sundance Square Annex of the Modern Art Museum of Fort Worth. Known as the Modern at Sundance Square, the facility was a return to downtown, the original home of the museum, which opened in 1892. Cal paused to take in the outline of a dancer that made up one of the neon paneled pieces at Caravan of Dreams, a nightclub that regularly featured nationally and regionally known performers. They popped into the lobby of a movie theater adorned with the skyline of a pretend city.

"I like this," Cal said, clasping Meredith's hand as they went on walking. She recklessly tightened her fingers around his. She took him past an outdoor coffeehouse jammed with a lunch crowd, pointed out the small museum devoted to Frederic Remington and Charles Russell pieces, then turned into a door under a sign that declared "Ragin' Cajun." The Ragin' Cajun himself, Mr. Lémieux, came forward to greet her.

"Meredith, it's good to see you," he said. "How is your father? A pleasure to meet you, Mr. Bonner. Come along, sit over here." He was French Canadian and spoke with a choppy accent. A small man with thinning dark hair and a pencil mustache, he had a colorful background. He'd had occasion once to visit a friend in the Crystal Creek jail, and after a couple of hours he and Meredith's dad had become fast friends. Everybody who came into contact with Mr. Lémieux became his friend. Meredith grinned at him and took the chair he pulled out for her. Cal looked a little befuddled, not quite so in control anymore. Meredith was pleased.

Mr. Lémieux didn't wait for them to order. He brought *étouffé*, steaming bowls of gumbo, crayfish pie, and his famous Opelousas-style red beans and rice. Cal gave the crayfish pie a doubtful look, but took a bite anyway. Meredith went after the gumbo, finding that her unsettling morning had made her quite ravenous. Cal examined the *étouffé* quizzically, then he glanced at the walls covered with customer business cards and Cajun Pride banners. The jukebox wailed a Cajun French song. Shrugging a little, Cal tried the *étouffé*.

A while later he loosened his tie and leaned back with a satisfied expression. "This place might not be much to look at, but the food is excellent."

"It's the best Cajun cooking this side of Louisiana," Meredith said.

"I wish I'd discovered it sooner."

"You're still planning on leaving, then?" Meredith kept her tone light.

"Maybe sooner than I expected." He traced a fork over the checkered tablecloth. "My father was at the Saturday night wine tasting. Seems he recently acquired a large advertising firm in San Francisco, and he wants me to run it."

"What about France?" Meredith asked in surprise. "You said you had an airplane ticket on hold."

"I'm still considering that, but that could take a while. I've come up with some other possibilities, too. Like buying the *Chronicle* from Sunmedia, going independent, getting away from my father altogether. His idea of what I should do with my life and mine don't always mesh. Sunmedia is his bat and ball, and I'm not sure I want to play his game anymore. There's a lot I could do at the *Chronicle*, besides installing a computer system. I especially like the advertising end of it, and I'm convinced the paper could eventually grow into a daily." Cal's expressive face came alive as he talked. "I want to make it on my own, Meredith. As Cal Bonner, not one of *the* Bonners, if that makes any sense.''

She listened to him, his enthusiasm catching hold of her. He was a good and decent man, surprisingly idealistic behind the cynical front he sometimes put up. Meredith felt an odd thickness in her throat, and wished suddenly that she could share his plans. She concentrated on refolding her napkin. ''It makes a lot of sense, Cal. But I don't see how a San Francisco advertising company will fit in.''

''It would be a good step for my career—I can't ignore that.''

''Cynthia likes the idea, I'm sure.''

Cal looked across at her. He was not exactly smiling, but his mouth was curved a little. ''Of course she likes it. It wasn't a coincidence that my father was there that night. She brought him along. She's trying to be subtle about it, but she thinks I should go on to bigger and better.''

''So you admit it!'' Meredith exclaimed triumphantly. ''Cynthia is full of plots. She—''

''Hold on, Meredith. Stop exaggerating. That's just the way Cynthia is. She's always thinking in terms of business deals, each one bolder than the last. It's one of the things that makes her so successful.''

Meredith took a bite of the tutti-frutti ice cream that Mr. Lémieux had placed before her. ''Maybe there are other kinds of success,'' she said. ''Buy the *Chronicle* or open your own advertising firm. Forget about everything else!''

His fork made a forceful pattern of squares on the tablecloth. ''Life looks pretty simple to you, doesn't it? As a matter of fact, my life was simple until you came crashing into it. I was going along just fine, living in a world I could understand, even if it wasn't perfect. I don't always agree with my father, but I understand him, and I understand women with the same drive and ambition as Cynthia Campbell. But you, Meredith, you're in a different world entirely. One you conjured up yourself. It's full of colors and dreams and memories but not a single practicality.''

Meredith watched her ice cream melt. Cal didn't sound very approving of her. It seemed that Cynthia represented his type of woman: sophisticated, successful, wielding business power with flair. He was right—Meredith wasn't like that. She had her own style and she'd always been proud of it before. Now she found herself wishing intensely that she could be powerful, take the corporate world by storm. Maybe then she, too, would have Cal's admiration.

It was shameful, this craving need to please him. She despised the need, and yet it grew stronger every day. She had to fight it with whatever weapons she had.

"I'll never stop believing in dreams," she declared. "Impractical dreams that don't have a thing to do with money or prestige. You have a few of those yourself, Cal."

"I didn't until I met you. You have that affect on me."

"Maybe that's good. Everybody needs a dream."

"All this is making my life a lot more complicated than it used to be."

Meredith pushed her bowl of ice cream away. "And Cynthia's way is less complicated," she said. "Safer. You'll go for bigger and better and play in the Bonner park."

Cal hooked an arm over the back of his chair. "I'll consider the San Francisco deal, yes. Because I want to.

But maybe I'll use that airplane ticket to France, or I might decide I like being a big fish in a small pond and buy the *Chronicle*. Then again, maybe I'll open my own advertising firm right here in Sundance Square. That way I could eat lunch at the Ragin' Cajun everyday. I don't know what I'm going to do, Meredith. When the time comes, Cynthia won't make the decision for me, and neither will my father.''

''Well, that's all I want,'' Meredith said hotly. ''To make my own decisions, without interference from you or Cynthia Campbell.''

''Your case is entirely different, Meredith. You need structure, otherwise you'll lose the freedom that's so important to you. New Dimensions will help you keep hold of your dreams. Don't you see that? I'm going to arrange another meeting with Cynthia so we can really talk about this.''

''You know what I think?'' she exclaimed. ''I think you're trying to push me into this thing with New Dimensions because you're at a crossroads in your own life. You don't have the answer for yourself yet, so you think you'll come up with one for me. Well, you don't need to bother. Solve your own problems, rich boy, not mine!''

''We made a deal,'' he said, his voice unyielding. ''You accepted the terms and you can't back out of them now.''

''You're forgetting something. I could never consider a decision this major without talking to Kayanne. She's as much a part of Grant Designs as I am, and Bo, too.''

''I agree with you. This opportunity is theirs, too, and we'll want their imput.'' His affability was deceptive, Meredith thought darkly. ''Go ahead, talk to them, by all means,'' he went on. ''Then we'll set up a time for you and me to meet with Cynthia.''

There seemed nothing more to say. Cal was the kind of man who always needed to be in charge, and he still had everything just the way he wanted it. He still had all the power in this relationship. They stared at each other across the table, and Meredith struggled to keep herself from being swirled into the depths of his eyes. Their intensity shook her.

''Agreed, Meredith?'' he said softly.

''You know you haven't left me any choice! I'll talk to Kayanne and Bo.'' She scraped back her chair and marched up to the cash register, pulling loose bills out of her pocket.

''Don't be absurd,'' Cal said beside her. ''I'm paying.''

''It was a business lunch. I'll pay.''

''Of course it was a business lunch. I'm your financial adviser, which makes you my client.''

''You're my client.''

''We didn't talk about interior decorating. Besides, technically that's my money you're throwing around.''

Mr. Lémieux came up to the register and settled the dispute. ''It's on the house, Meredith. No, you can't change my mind. Just say hello to your papa for me.''

Meredith felt deflated, but held out until Cal pocketed his money first. They walked in grim silence back to his car six blocks away. They drove silently all the way to Crystal Creek and parked in his driveway behind the battered furniture van that Kayanne and Bo drove for Grant Designs. Still without speaking, they sat in the car under the shade of an oak. Sunlight flickered through the leaves, warming the windshield. Cal's hand rested on the gearshift knob; Meredith glanced down at his strong fingers, which could be so surprisingly gentle. She swung her door open.

"I won't keep you any longer. Good-bye, Cal." She was halfway around the car when she almost bumped smack into him.

"Don't you have to be someplace?" she asked stiffly.

"Yes."

"So . . . good-bye, then."

"Good-bye."

They stood looking at each other for one long, sunshine-shimmering moment. Then Cal strode back around the car, climbed in, slammed the door, and roared off.

Meredith sat down on the porch steps, watching dolefully as one of the carpenters carried some boards to the back of the house. She thought about Cynthia's exotic beauty and graceful style; she thought about her own freckled nose and the way she bumped into things because she was always in a hurry and never looked where she was going. And suddenly she wanted very badly to surrender herself to Cal. To be swept up by his compelling strength. She'd follow wherever he led her, even if that meant joining Cynthia Campbell's camp at New Dimensions.

She jumped up, reminding herself that she was fighting a battle with Cal. A fierce and desperate one. She couldn't afford to lose either her freedom or her heart to him. The best thing was to begin aligning her forces right away; she was going to need every bit of help she could muster.

She headed into the house to find her allies, Kayanne and Bo.

Chapter Eight

"Sounds like a great idea to me, Mere," Bo said, a glob of periwinkle-blue paint flying off his brush as he waved it about in the corner bedroom upstairs. "That Bonner guy knows what he's talking about. We'd be making a ton of money if we joined New Dimensions."

"Since when are you interested in money?" Meredith asked, her eyebrows drawing together.

"I could save up more for college in the fall," he explained. "So when I start classes I can afford to cut my work hours down."

"Bo, you wouldn't really be working for me any-more," Meredith said. "You'd be an employee of New Dimensions and they might not be so flexible about your schedule."

Bo pushed up the brim of his baseball cap. "Maybe I'll work my way up in the company," he said. "Then I wouldn't have to go to college at all."

"Don't you even think about that, Bo Grant!" Meredith said, pointing her finger in a menacing gesture. "Of course you're going to college. That isn't even open for discussion." She turned to Kayanne. "You haven't said anything yet. What do you think about the New Dimensions deal?"

Kayanne set her paintbrush aside and hooked a strand of hair behind her ear. "I think it could be the answer to all our problems, Mere," she said seriously. "I can't tell you how worried I've been about our finances. It's not just Mrs. Lipscomb, either. We're suffering a general trend toward chaos. We need to control it and at the same time inject some growth into the business."

"You sound like you've been hanging out with Cal Bonner and his crowd," Meredith muttered. "I thought you liked being independent, Kayanne. Setting your own schedule, taking off when you needed the time . . ."

"Those are all the things *you* like, Mere," Kayanne said apologetically. Her voice started traveling up and down the scale the way it did when she was nervous. "I need order in my life, Mere. I want to know when I'll get my next paycheck. It's nothing persoanl. Really, it isn't. I'm sorry, but I have college tuition coming up, too, and a new apartment to pay for, and I think if I had to move back home I'd go bananas." Kayanne's cheeks had turned pink; she always colored when she was agitated.

Meredith studied her sister ruefully. "Don't apologize, Kayanne. I understand, and you aren't asking for very much."

"You're not angry?" Kayanne asked, still anxious.

"Of course not. I just have to do a lot more thinking about New Dimensions, that's all. I'm glad you both told me how you felt." Meredith went downstairs to the library. She stood at the mantelpiece, feeling peculiarly alone. It seemed that life was more complicated than she wanted to believe. All along she'd been living her own dream, thinking it was right for Kayanne and Bo, too. That had been selfish, especially when they had been so loyal. They had sacrificed a lot to keep the business going; how could she deny them the opportunities they would find at New Dimensions?

At the same time, how could she deny herself? Yes, it might be a relief to have a regular paycheck, to know she could afford to replace the van when it wheezed its last. But how would she be able to survive in a place like New Dimensions? To use Kayanne's words, she'd go bananas!

Finding no answers to her questions, she turned to the old house for solace and comfort. She placed a hand on the lovely onyx marble of the mantelpiece, pressing against the smooth, cool surface until the confusion of her thoughts began to quiet down. Then she slipped off her blazer and rolled up her sleeves. Ignoring the fact that she was wearing her best skirt, she went to work stripping the rest of the wainscoting. Somehow she would figure out what to do about New Dimensions.

Her first strategy was simple: she stalled. The next morning Cal called her twice while she was working at his house, pushing her to set a time for the second meeting with Cynthia. Meredith changed the subject repeatedly. She argued with him—and finally she just hung up on him. Both times. She was irked when he showed up in person an hour or so after the last confrontation.

He was in a good mood, as if he enjoyed having a receiver slammed down in his ear. Dropping his jacket on the newel post, he took Meredith into his arms. It was a dangerous thing to do, since she was holding a hammer and a packet of nails and wasn't feeling especially friendly toward him. But he waltzed her through the hallway with expert ease, humming one of those old Fred Astaire-Ginger Rogers movie tunes. Cal was a marvelous dancer, and his arms were strong and warm. Meredith leaned against him, breathless by the time they ended up back at the newel post. He was still humming in her ear, sending delicious vibrations all through her. Then he kissed the pulse at her temple and stepped back. She almost dropped the hammer on her toe.

"Isn't that better than arguing?" he asked.

"Definitely," she said, but she narrowed her eyes at him with suspicion. "What are you up to, Cal? I don't like this fast change in tactics. You're trying to soften me up, aren't you?"

"I wanted to see you, Meredith. Spur of the moment—that's it. Ellen's covering for me at the newspaper the rest of the day . . . and I have no idea why I'm doing this." He was beginning to look disgruntled, like a man waking from dream to reality. But Meredith felt buoyant, as if he'd whirled her around the floor again. He had disrupted his entire schedule—all for her!

"I was just tacking in some baseboards," she said happily. "The carpenters finished up yesterday, but they forgot a few details—not that I blame them. The one named Tony has been pretty distracted by Kayanne. She finally said she'd go to the movies with him." Meredith knew she was babbling; she never knew how Cal was going to affect her. He didn't seem to be listening to her, though. He looked at the empty paint cans scattered about, the box full of doorknobs that had been pushed into a corner, the dust rags draped over the stair rail.

"My life is like this house," he muttered. "Everything out of place. Are you ever going to finish one room? Just one room? Is that too much to ask?"

Meredith tried to distract him. She pointed to a corner that was very neat and tidy at the moment. "I'm thinking there should be a grandfather clock over there. What do you think?"

Cal gave her suggestion some thought. "That might not be a bad idea," he conceded. "Not bad at all." He turned back to Meredith. "We'll go buy a clock right now. What do you say? A grandfather clock that chimes every fifteen minutes, until you want to stuff a sock in it. Can't have a house without one of those.''

She stared at him. This was much more than she'd hoped for. ''Are you serious? That's really what you want to do?''

''Meredith, I have a limited capacity for this kind of thing. Don't press your luck by making me think about it too much.''

''Don't think about it at all, then!'' She ran upstairs to tell Kayanne she was leaving, then hurried out to join Cal at the Jaguar. He opened the car door for her and gratefully she sank into the luxurious leather seat.

''I know just where to go,'' she said, giving him directions. She glanced at him as he drove. ''Listen, I'm sorry I yelled at you on the phone.''

''Are you sorry you called me a jerk?'' he asked gravely. ''I really am trying to come up with a good deal for you, Meredith. I'm negotiating with Cynthia so that she'll give you all the freedom you need.''

Meredith sighed. He was changing his tactics on purpose, she was sure of that. ''I already told you that Kayanne and Bo are interested,'' she said. ''But can you guarantee that they'd both still be part of Grant Designs, just as they are now? And there's something even more important. They should have promotion opportunities at New Dimensions.''

''Cynthia will be fair about that. You don't need to worry. New Dimensions rewards hard work and initiative.''

It all sounded so logical, so suitable, and yet Meredith's instincts still warned her to run from New Dimensions as fast as she could. Cynthia Campbell was not offering any of this out of the kindness of her heart.

By now they were approaching the Dallas city limits, and at Meredith's direction Cal drove to a shabby, down-at-the-heels area under the freeway where tourists seldom ventured.

"Are you sure you know where you're going?" Cal asked skeptically.

"Sure. Pull up over there."

Cal did as he was told, stopping in front of a dingy little store on a side street.

"I thought we were going to a department store or something like that," he protested.

"A department store?" Meredith echoed in disbelief.

"How else do you buy furniture? You need a clock, you go to the clock department. You buy the clock."

"Good grief, you don't shop for furniture the way you do for shoes. You have to know how to browse."

"I don't browse. We're going to a department store."

Meredith swung out of the Jaguar. "Relax, rich boy. You're going to enjoy this." Before he could say anything more, she led him into the shop. It was a jumble of dusty paintings and books, murky wood carvings, old chests and bookcases, tarnished jewelry heaped in cracked bowls.

"This is junk," Cal grumbled, just as a tall, skinny old man materialized from the clutter.

"My dear Meredith," he murmured in a voice that was papery thin. "I haven't seen you in a long time. Where have you been hiding yourself?"

"Oh, Mr. Vickers, I've been working on the most marvelous house. You'd love it. It's over in Crystal Creek. Maybe you've heard of it. It's called the House of the Seasons."

"Ah, yes. Crystal Creek is an interesting area. Fascinating history. Fascinating." Mr. Vickers smoothed a few wisps of hair across the bald spot on top of his head. His milk-blue eyes took on a faraway expression. "Crystal Creek was once a thriving community. Many prominent people made their home there. When the railroad bypassed the town, they abandoned their lovely homes for better ones in the city."

Meredith shook her head emphatically. "The House of the Seasons wasn't treated like that, Mr. Vickers. The same family lived there for years and years, until they were all gone, and I'm sure they loved it."

"I'm glad to hear that. Houses should be loved, not simply lived in. Unfortunately, that doesn't happen often enough, especially with the older homes. Pardon me for saying this, my dear, but your generation are the worst offenders. I had a very dear friend who passed away recently. She had a baroque Mediterranean mansion. Great mystique. Her husband built it in 1925, and she lived there from the time of her marriage, at the age of seventeen, until the day she died at eighty-seven. The house sits on four-and-a-half acres of land, and she left it all to her only child. A son, who promptly sold it to some company that's planning on renovating. It's going to be a restaurant, with an addition for a hotel!"

The scenario sounded familiar, and Meredith ventured a guess. "Was the name of the company New Dimensions?"

Mr. Vickers smoothed his wisps of hair in the other direction. "Come to think of it, yes. That is the name. I'm almost sure. I don't even like to think about it. That beautiful home. So many memories." He sighed nostalgically.

"I know what you mean," Meredith said.

Cal cleared his throat. "I thought we were shopping for a grandfather clock," he remarked.

"We are," Meredith said. "Mr. Vickers, this is Cal Bonner, my client. Cal, this is Mr. Vickers, who can tell you anything and everything you want to know about clocks."

"I believe I do have a few in the back somewhere," Mr. Vickers said, gesturing vaguely. "A few months ago I spotted a cuckoo clock behind one of the bookshelves, but I haven't seen it lately."

Cal was tensing like a spring wound too tightly, and Meredith put a hand on his arm. "I hate to tell you this," she said. "We're going to . . . browse. Trust me and see what happens."

Cal groaned, but followed her further into the shop. It was long and narrow, with more and more treasures piling up toward the back. Cal poked his foot at a rolled-up Persian carpet and fought his way around a china cabinet.

"How can you find anything in here?" he hissed at Meredith. "There's probably a few forgotten customers moldering back here."

"Just be ready for anything," Meredith instructed him as she went to inspect a table carved out of tulipwood.

She poked and sifted and scrounged through the entire shop. Now and then she'd catch a glimpse of Cal, mysterious rolls of parchment under his arm or his tie flung back over his shoulder as he rummaged through boxes. He reappeared at the front of the shop while Meredith was consulting with Mr. Vickers over the counter. She hadn't stumbled upon a grandfather clock; she contented herself with other finds.

"Let's see . . . we're taking the writing desk," she said. "And the Shaker table and chairs, and the bureau. Oh, and that pile of sheet music."

"Wait a minute," Cal protested. "What do we need that for?"

"We just do," Meredith said patiently. "There are some wonderful old songs in there. Now, Mr. Vickers, I think that's all. We'll carry a few things with us, but Kayanne and Bo will be around with the van tomorrow—"

"The armchairs," Cal muttered.

Meredith turned to him. "What?"

"The armchairs over there. We're taking those. And that set of candlesticks."

Meredith raised her eybrows at the hideous Victorian candelabra, but thought better of arguing with him. It wasn't difficult to prod Cal to the next little shop she had in mind . . . and the next one after that. The possibility of a grandfather clock beckoned them on.

They scrounged and explored together. Right in the middle of a heated discussion over the usefulness of a battered washboard, Meredith realized how happy she was. Simply and purely happy. She was sharing her world with Cal. And she wanted to share so much more of it with him—regardless of the tortured expression on his face.

Eventually he took off his tie and left his jacket tossed carelessly in the backseat of the car. The front of his expensive shirt grew dusty from rummaging among tables and cabinets and bookshelves.

"That mirror. Those rugs," he said. Meredith began to notice a glazed look in his eyes.

"Maybe we shouldn't take all the rugs," she hinted.

"All of them," he said grimly.

She shrugged. "I suppose Kayanne and Bo won't mind making a few extra trips. The overhead will kill me, though, because they'll stop for ice cream or pizza every few hours. My baby brother is six feet, four inches tall and still growing. He needs lots of nourishment to load furniture. Kayanne always has to go on a diet after she's spent a few days working with him.''

Cal didn't answer. There was an alarming glitter in his eyes now as he advanced on a shelf of flowerpots. Meredith recognized the look, and decided it was time to take action.

''Kind of addictive, isn't it?'' she commented, and led him out of the last store.

He blinked, glancing around in the sunlight. He still didn't look quite himself. He took several deep breaths. ''Are we ever going to find that clock? . . . I can't remember if I bought that model train set.''

Meredith laughed. ''Yes, you did, and I think you'd better come with me before you OD on browsing!''

There was a taco stand at the end of the block with small picnic tables placed in front of it. They split the four-chicken-tacos-for-a-dollar special and shared an order of nachos, washed down with large Pepsis.

''Feel better?'' Meredith asked Cal as they gathered up cups, empty boxes, and a litter of napkins and tossed them in a nearby garbage can.

He looked at her with a level, speculative glance. ''What the devil happened to me?''

''It's a common malady known as browser's syndrome. Very curable, if caught in the early stages. After that . . .'' She let the words trail off into a teasing shrug.

They walked back to Cal's car with their arms bumping companionably, and Meredith gave herself over to the joy of being with Cal. Surely this once it couldn't hurt to let down her defenses. The beauty of the day practically demanded it. Dallas summer on its best behavior—the sky brushed with fingers of white cloud, but blue high up in its vault; bright and warm but not too hot; a light breeze stirring around them. She was wearing her good perfume, the Opium, and she suddenly thought of it with a tingle of pleasure.

"Where to now?" Cal asked once they were settled in the Jaguar.

"I'd love to do some more browsing, if you're up to it."

"Just point the way."

She did, and they ended up in Grapevine, a wonderful community located halfway between Dallas and Fort Worth. There were more than seventy-five faithfully restored homes and commercial buildings, and housed in many of those treasures were antique and specialty shops. Cal's eyes began to glaze over again as they explored Grapevine's historic Main Street, then swung over to the Torlan cabin in Liberty Park. It was a marvelous log cabin that was at least a hundred years old.

"It was somewhere right around here that Sam Houston and members of the Republic of Texas met in 1844 to sign a treaty with a delegation of Indian tribes," she told him. "Under the oaks of what was known then as Grape Vine Springs."

"Very interesting." His fingers caressed the nape of her neck, and she found she wasn't able to think very logically or clearly.

"Yes, I thought so," she managed to say. "They have a beautiful fireworks display here on the Fourth of July."

"Maybe we could see it together this year."

She smiled at him, relishing his words.

They didn't talk for a time, enclosed in their own magic, even though a crowd milled around them. Cal put his arm around her, his hand warm on her shoulder. "Meredith, I have an idea about New Dimensions, and I want you to listen to it."

"Not now, Cal, please—"

"We've had such a good morning," he said. "We should be able to talk sensibly about this now."

She stiffened. "I was right, then. This was a new strategy of yours. You thought you'd get me in a good mood by shopping for a clock. I'll bet you don't even *want* a grandfather clock!"

He looked harassed. "It was your idea to begin with, remember?"

"But the way you took the day off . . . you had something in mind, some way to soften me up." She was rigid with indignation now. Cal maneuvered her around so that she had to face him.

"Listen to me, Meredith," he commanded. "Believe it or not, I did want to be with you today. You . . . do something to me."

She stood at arm's length from him, unable to trust his words.

"Blast it all, Cal Bonner! You planned all this. Don't try to deny it. I was really beginning to think today was special. That we could be together without you trampling all over me."

"You do have a gift for exaggeration, Meredith. Okay, I thought it wouldn't hurt for me to be a little more flexible and spend some time doing things your way. But I didn't stay up all night hatching a plot. I just had an urge to see you. Is that so hard to believe?"

She didn't care what he told her, or how he tried to explain it away. "You're just like my father—loud and bossy!"

"I'm not loud—"

"Yes, you are, and if you were trying to charm me, you did an excellent job of it. You had me going there for a while. Too bad it all backfired. You spent a whole lot of money on furniture you didn't want—just so I'd melt in gratitude and do anything you said."

He brought her toward him and she had to plant both hands on his chest to keep a distance. He scowled down at her.

"You're right, I didn't want two lamps that need rewiring or a treadle sewing machine that won't treadle. But I saw the way you looked at all that junk—like you'd just discoverd a 1919 Honus Wagner baseball card. So I bought the stuff. I got carried away. How much criminal intent can you read into that?"

She was trembling inside, wanting to believe that the morning had been special for him, too. A time to be with her and savor her company, nothing more. She took a deep breath.

"Prove yourself, then," she challenged. "Tell me right now that we won't talk about New Dimensions or Cynthia Campbell, not once the whole rest of the day."

His eyes were stony now. "I'm not going to try passing a test for you, Meredith. I told you the truth. On the spur of the moment I decided I wanted to spend some time with you. And yes, I thought it would help our relationship if I showed you I could give a little, too. But I've come up with a compromise on New Dimensions and you're going to listen to it now."

She kept her hands splayed across his chest, resisting him. But he held her captive with little effort.

"Cynthia already has a client who wants her house redecorated," he said. "It's supposed to be one of your first assignments, but I think I can convince Cynthia to put it on a trial basis. You'd find out how you like working for New Dimensions before actually signing on. Nothing could be more reasonable."

It *was* reasonable, and Meredith found that especially

irritating. She relaxed her vigilance for a moment, arms slackening as she tried to think of a rebuttal. Cal took advantage of this, his own arms tightening around her until she was cradled against him.

"I'm only asking you to do an experiment with New Dimensions," he said next to her cheek.

"I won't—I won't agree to anything under these circumstances . . ." His mouth was leaving a trail of flickering heat across her skin, and she couldn't think straight. A balding man with wire-rimmed spectacles looked on with interest, fingering his camera.

"We make a good picture together," Cal murmured in her ear. "And I'm handing over all the money you need, don't forget. I'm living up to my end of the bargain and you have to do the same. Say cheese."

She clenched her fists, but they were wedged securely between her body and Cal's. She arched her head back and stared at him.

"You have me entirely under control, don't you?" she asked bitterly. "But that's all I'm giving New Dimensions—a trial, just like you said. Nothing more!"

Cal released her, but not before the camera had clicked. It was a Polaroid, and a moment later the man handed Meredith the photograph that had scrolled out of it. He peered at her over his spectacles.

"Have a good day, Miss." He walked off jauntily.

Meredith looked down at the photograph as the colors deepened. There she and Cal were, locked in what appeared to be a lovers' embrace. But they were glowering at each other, and that ruined the effect somewhat.

Meredith didn't know whether to laugh or cry. Maybe she should be doing both, because it was preserved forever now—this moment of capitulation to Cal.

Chapter Nine

Meredith climbed the ladder to Cal's attic, grumbling to herself. Everything was moving too fast with New Dimensions, for once again Cal hadn't wasted any time. It was only yesterday that he'd forced her to agree to a trial, yet he'd already arranged everything with Cynthia. Just now he had phoned from the newspaper to inform Meredith that her first command performance would be this very morning; she was to be at a certain Overbrook address at precisely ten o'clock.

She had banged down the receiver in Cal's ear, again.

She had only a couple of hours of liberty. She knelt before the clothes chest, lifting up the lid and taking out the lavender ball gown. She had brought along a generous supply of tissue paper, and carefully began wrapping the gown to protect it. Her hand lingered on the soft folds; she remembered clearly the way Cal had kissed her here. The emotions of that day had not dissipated, but still clung to the musty, closed-in air. Already she and Cal were building too many memories together.

She fished the Polaroid photograph out of her pocket and held it up to the light. She looked at Cal's rumpled hair, his obstinate jaw. He was staring at Meredith as if the very force of his gaze would compel her to submit to him. His sleeve was rolled up above the elbow, showing the strong muscles of his forearm as he held her close.

Her fingers tightened on the photograph, ready to crumple it. But that would be an exercise in futility. Even if she cut it into a hundred pieces and threw them all away, Cal would still dominate her thoughts. She tucked the photograph safely back into her pocket.

The other dresses in the chest required her attention. She smoothed out the wrinkles as best she could and wrapped each gown in tissue. It was an enjoyable task and she stretched it out as long as possible. Toward the bottom of the chest she found a cruet, a cameo ring, a strand of pearls, a mesh evening bag, and a book with a plain blue cover . . . a diary. She controlled her eagerness as she opened it, for the pages were brittle and coming loose from the binding. An inscription was written in ornate script on the flyleaf: *To Ima Rose on her eighteenth birthday—God bless you and may all these pages be filled with happy dreams.* It was signed *Aunt Jenny.*

Oh, this was treasure indeed. Ima Rose Benjamine, the last person to live in the House of the Seasons. Meredith sat cross-legged in front of the small fan-shaped window so that sunlight would stream across the diary. Her pleated pants would be all grimy now, but she didn't care. Dust motes settled around her as she began to read.

The first entries in the book were about parties and the boys who courted Ima Rose. Ima's handwriting was bold and impatient, so scribbled in places that it was barely legible. She'd obviously been a restless girl who wanted something more than the endless parties chaperoned by her parents. She wanted adventure, and one day she found it. Meredith bent her head closer to the diary, scanning the words that had been dashed off so excitedly:

July 5, 1917

Something wonderful happened last night! It all started as a lark. The Andersons' Fourth of July party was ever so stodgy, even for them, and I persuaded Patricia to sneak off with me to the canteen. The place was marvelous, decorated with red, white, and blue crepe paper streamers, and dozens of balloons of the same patriotic colors. The music was lively, jazz, mostly. Patricia was as nervous as a long-tailed cat in a room full of rocking chairs, and she nearly fainted when a young officer, a captain, asked me to dance—and I said yes! Oh, how dashing he looked in that Air Corps uniform. I could scarcely breathe, much less talk, as he waltzed me around the dance floor. He just looked and looked at me. He has very intense, very blue eyes. And he dances like a dream. That's what it felt like, a dream.

Patricia left, scandalized. But she won't tell on me. Edward and I had punch, and later took a walk along the creek. He has curly brown hair, and dimples. All he ever wanted to do is be a pilot. I told him I wanted to be a journalist. He said I'd be the prettiest reporter the world had ever seen. He's shipping out soon—but I refuse to think about that now.

July 10

Mama and Papa are in a dreadful temper. They caught me sneaking into the house last night. Edward made it safely over the hedge, but they know all about him now. It's for the best. They can't stop us. I love him, and I know he loves me.

July 16

Edward's unit shipped out yesterday. I know he would have contacted me if he could have. Maybe he tried to. If he'd sent a note Mama or Papa would surely have intercepted it, and I'd never know. I must remember to go by the post office first thing each morning, before Papa. I know Edward will write as soon as he can.

August 9

Still no letter from Edward. But I know he hasn't forgotten me—no matter what Mama says. Is it possible she was ever in love? I don't think so. There is a war going on, after all, and Edward is part of that awful mess. I pray for his safe return each and every night. I know he will write to me as soon as he can. And, God willing, he'll come back for me.

There were no more entries in the diary. Meredith examined the pages again, saddened by the realization that Ima Rose had gone to her grave as the spinster "Miss Ima." So obviously Edward never came back for her, for one reason or another. Was he a casuality of the Great War? Or was he a rogue in uniform having one last fling? Or both? Was he the reason Ima Rose never married?

Meredith leaned back against the wall, her hands wrapped around the diary. The mild winters and dry climate brought Texas some of the principal training camps during World War I, including Camp Sam Houston in Crystal Creek. It was gone long before she was born, but Meredith knew her great-grandfather had been stationed there for a time, before shipping overseas. Was it possible that he'd known Ima Rose's Edward? There was no way of finding out now; her great-grandfather had died the year she was born. Besides, she didn't even have a last name for Edward.

It seemed that the House of the Seasons had known many emotions—heartbreak and despair, but surely happiness, too. Perhaps Edward ended up as the one with the broken heart; he might have returned and Ima Rose had already launched her journalism career, creating a happy, productive life on her own. Surely that was more important than anything else. Memories should never get in the way of dreams. How could she have forgotten so quickly? She, Meredith Grant, who had always made her own way in the world and who had trembled before nobody and no situation. Now look at her!

She had started to change inside, from the very first moment she met Cal. But she didn't want to change, didn't want to be as vulnerable as Ima Rose had been all those years ago.

Meredith glanced at her watch and grimaced. Her time had run out. She put Ima's diary back in the chest, laying the tissue-wrapped dresses on top of it. Then she climbed back down the ladder, brushed off her pants, and straightened the shoulders of her silk blouse. She was as ready as she'd ever be for her induction with New Dimensions.

She got in her van and cut across town to Highway 20, then to I-35, arriving at the Overbrook address in Dallas at five minutes to ten. She pulled into the drive of a Mediterranean-style villa. Cal's Jaguar was already parked there.

Meredith sat in her van for a moment, smoothing back wisps of windblown hair. Even Mrs. Lipscomb's sprawling Italianate brick-and-stucco design could not compare with this imposing mansion. Meredith suspected that her trial run with New Dimensions was going to be quite a job.

She slid out of the van, glancing about at the meticulous landscaping, at the series of flagstone walkways, terraces, and trees, including three-story crepe myrtles, dogwoods, and shrubbery that had been severely pruned. They looked like men who'd had their hair cut too short at the barber shop. The flowers in the garden were lined up in perfectly straight rows, as if measured out with a yardstick. Meredith wondered if unruly flowers were yanked up by the roots. She shuddered, then advanced up the steps.

The Spanish Colonial facade was glamorous and graceful, with its ivy-covered stucco and red tile roof. Before Meredith had a chance to ring the doorbell, the large door opened swiftly and silently. A young man in a butler's uniform gazed at her lugubriously.

"Yes, madam?"

"Hi there! How are you today?"

He gave her a suspicious glance.

"Um, I'm Meredith Grant," she said. "I have an appointment . . ."

"Of course. Please come in." He stood back, and Meredith entered the two-story foyer that offered hardwood flooring, parchment stucco walls, and an iron staircase. She skirted a monstrous round table, and followed the butler. His brown hair was cut to severe shortness, though one unmanageable shock stood up in back. Meredith wished she had a beach ball to bounce off his head. He was too young to behave so sedately.

Before she could reflect on this idea any further, Meredith found herself ushered into the drawning room. And

there was Cal talking to Cynthia Campbell, his head bent
toward her. Meredith bit her lip, feeling a stab of pure-
green animal jealousy. Then her mouth quirked wryly.
At least ''green'' was an appropriate word when thinking
about Cynthia. Today the woman was wearing a soft
emerald-green knit dress that outlined her curves, but not
blantantly; she looked feminine and businesslike at the
same time. She was also perfectly groomed. Meredith
suddenly became aware of the smudges still adorning her
trousers, and wondered if she had cobwebs in her hair
from Cal's attic. Oh, well, she liked cobwebs.

Cal was regarding her sardonically. Her heart pulsed
in her throat as she gazed back at him. Tension crackled
between them.

''My,'' Cynthia murmured. Meredith wrenched her
eyes away from Cal and tried to listen as Cynthia con-
tinued after a pause. ''Cal and I are both so glad that
you agreed to give New Dimensions a chance, Meredith.
I want to introduce you to your new client, Miss Annabelle Mohr.''

Meredith glanced about the room. The windows were
draped in dark-brown velvet; all the furniture was made
of heavy dark wood. Gradually her eyes discerned a very
small, very old woman perched on a huge antique sofa.
She gazed out fearfully as Cynthia led Meredith over to
her.

''I'm pleased to meet you,'' Meredith said, sitting at
the other end of the sofa. It was hard and uncomfortable,
but she sensed it would be best not to shift about. Annabelle Mohr looked like a sparrow that might go flut-
tering away at any sudden movement. Her gnarled hands
were plucking nervously at her brown taffeta gown; the
stiff material covered her primly from her fragile neck
to the tips of her toes. Her ice-white hair was dressed in

the elaborate fashion of bygone years, the coquettish ringlets and curls somehow fitting against the wrinkles of her face. She intrigued Meredith, most of all because she seemed so reluctant to have this meeting.

"Miss Mohr, why don't you tell me about your plans to redecorate your house," Meredith began, feeling her way cautiously.

But even this appeared to be too much for the woman. "Oh, dear . . . plans . . ." Annabelle's voice was like a rustle of dry leaves in an autumn wind. She said nothing more, her face looking pinched and worried.

Cynthia had taken a seat in a chair close by. "Yes, do tell us about your plans, Annabelle," she urged. "Annabelle's niece is quite thrilled about them, Meredith. Cecy Tulte—surely you've heard of her."

Meredith nodded absently; she'd seen the name a few times in the society columns. She waited patiently for Annabelle to speak.

"The furniture must go," Annabelle finally murmured. "Even though it has been in the family for years and years . . ." She patted her hand gently along the arm of the sofa.

"Oh, yes," Cynthia said. "Cecy has already chosen some glass tables and an organic sofa unit. Light and airy. She's encouraging Annabelle to go for an uncluttered look." Her gaze zeroed in on a bookcase that was crammed with knickknacks. Annabelle's small, gnarled hand lifted to her throat in a gesture of alarm.

Meredith examined the room again, making her own assessment. Most of the furniture consisted of massive, ornately carved Victorian pieces, ugly but in superb condition. The room was sumptuous but austere, and made Meredith want to speak in a low voice, surrounded as she was by expensive paintings, priceless antiques, profusions of marble and gold trimmings. All standing like shrine-offering treasures to some unseen, unnamed god. The simple noise caused by heels clicking across the flooring was catalyst enough to set off a general alert.

Meredith's gaze came to rest on Cal. He was standing at one of the floor-to-ceiling windows where the draperies had been pulled aside, and his tall figure was silhouetted by the light. She couldn't see his features, but she could tell his attention was focused on her. She turned back to Annabelle.

"Miss Mohr," she said, "I want you to forget about Cecy and the rest of us for a minute. Just tell me what you'd like to see here in this room."

"Why . . . I don't really know."

"Meredith," Cynthia said, a warning edge to her voice.

Meredith ignored her. "I think I sense what the problem is, Miss Mohr," she went on. "You don't want your house turned upside down all of a sudden. But have you thought of a few new touches here and there? Perhaps that little rug in front of that beautiful fireplace could be replaced. Something claret-colored, maybe. And how about a few lovely vases to display your flowers from the garden?"

Annabelle's brown eyes were suddenly hopeful. "Yes . . . yes, that would do nicely. I'd much prefer that. If only Cecy would listen."

"Just tell her exactly what you want, and exactly what you don't want," Meredith said cheerfully.

Cynthia stood up, anger flashing across her face. But a second later she was composed again. "Annabelle, I think it would be a good idea if I started showing Meredith the rest of the house. We won't take too long." She waited for Meredith to follow her out to the hall, then motioned the way to another drab room and closed the door.

"What happened just now with Annabelle was really my fault," she said pleasantly. "I made a judgment error by not explaining the situation fully to you beforehand. Cecy Tulte is one of New Dimensions' most influential investors. When she told me that she was helping her aunt redecorate this house, I promised to do all I could to assist her. As you can see, Annabelle is quite indecisive—she needs the guidance Cecy's providing. I don't want to undermine that."

Meredith ran her hand over a lace tablecloth, which was obviously a family heirloom; perhaps Cecy wanted to get rid of it, too.

"I can't agree with you, Cynthia," Meredith said firmly. "It looks to me like Cecy's forcing her aunt into a decorating job the poor woman doesn't want. Annabelle Mohr would be lost if her house were completely done over. She needs stability and continuity."

"You've barely met her! How can you possibly know anything about her?"

"It's obvious how she feels. You could see it yourself, if you'd only open your eyes."

Cynthia gestured at a lamp shade with a rotting fringe of brownish red. "Look around you, Meredith. Surely you realize this whole place is pathetic."

"Given a free hand, I would change just about everything," Meredith said. "But that's not the point. I have to respect the needs of my clients. With Miss Mohr I would move very, very slowly. I'm sure she does want some change . . . but just a little."

Cynthia rested her hand on an ornate captain's chair. She went on being pleasant. "I think I had better repeat this to you, Meredith. Cecy Tulte is one of New Dimensions' most valued investors and I don't want to alienate her.''

''Does this house belong to her?''

''No, of course not. It belongs to Annabelle.''

''I suppose. Cecy will inherit it someday,'' Meredith said reflectively. ''That would explain things. She's just getting a head start on her own decorating ideas.''

The anger sparked back into Cynthia's face. ''Her motives are none of your concern! At New Dimensions that's another thing you'll have to remember.''

''What I won't do, Cynthia, is help Cecy Tulte make her own aunt miserable.''

''Think about what you're really saying,'' Cynthia instructed coldly. ''Think about it carefully and perhaps you'll want to revise it.''

''I'm saying that Cecy Tulte has no right to take over this house before it's actually hers.''

Cynthia paced among the heavy, elaborate pieces of furniture that probably had not been moved in generations. She emanated a tension that jarred in this room where time had stopped.

''I wish Cal could hear you the way I do,'' she said. ''Somehow you believe that you should never have to compromise. That takes a certain arrogance, but Cal thinks you're so independent, so unique. He wanted to make sure you didn't lose any freedom at New Dimensions. I've tried to accommodate him on that. I really have.''

''Why?'' Meredith demanded. ''Why do you even want Grant Designs at all? I wish you'd explain that to me.''

Cynthia smiled contemptuously. ''It's very simple, Meredith. I knew that once you were at New Dimensions and competing in the real business world, Cal would see you're not so special, after all. Just a common, ordinary drudge like all the rest of them. You could never climb very far at New Dimensions. You see, it takes something truly exceptional to succeed in a corporation like that— an ability to follow the rules and at the same time reach higher than anyone else. You just don't have that.''

Meredith listened with quiet scorn. ''It was all a lie, then,'' she said. ''You didn't plan on giving any opportunities to Kayanne and Bo, the way you promised.''

''Of course I did, if they could prove they deserved those opportunities. My offer was legitimate—I do play fair. It's just that I knew you'd flounder eventually in spite of that, Meredith. I didn't expect it to be so soon, that's all.''

''I suppose you thought I'd be easier to control.''

''I prefer to say that I direct my employees. They're allowed plenty of responsibility as long as they don't do anything to harm the company. I'm known as a good boss. You would have found that to be true.''

Meredith shook her head in disbelief. ''You play games with people, Cynthia. You even play them with New Dimensions, using the company for your own private schemes.''

Cynthia's mouth constricted to a thin line of crimson, yet her beauty remained unmarred. When she spoke again, her voice was sharp and chilling, all the soft throatiness gone from it. ''I never jeopardize New Dimensions. Believe me, I'd like to keep you on so I could prove to Cal how ordinary you are. I'd really like to, but I won't. You're out of New Dimensions, Meredith. Out!''

''I never wanted in. I think you knew that. But I would have surprised you. I would have achieved my own kind of success.''

Cynthia seemed to be enjoying herself now. "Too bad we'll never know. And it's too bad we both want the same man."

Meredith recoiled from that last statement, but she kept her expression noncommittal. Cynthia watched her. "Don't be so reserved, Meredith," she said mockingly. "Why don't you admit you're in love with Cal?"

The words hit Meredith with a jolt. In love with Cal! That was the last thing she needed. She'd been struggling against it all along. She turned away, but Cynthia spoke again.

"Just remember, Meredith, I'm going to keep on fighting for Cal. I'll do whatever I can to have him."

Meredith swiveled back. Cynthia looked so striking with her scarlet mouth and flowing hair, her aura of self-confidence. Meredith refused to allow herself to feel inadequate. Not anymore. She had her own confidence.

"Watch out," Meredith said hotly. "If I ever decide to fight for Cal, you'll have a real opponent. Because to me he'd be more than just a prize for the winning—much more. He might like that for a change." She went to the door, flung it open, then strode down the hall, heels making a forceful tattoo over the marble floor. She didn't look back to see if Cynthia was following.

Cal regarded Meredith speculatively when she entered the drawing room to make her farewells to Annabelle. The old woman held out a hand. "I hope you'll come to see me again," she said. "And we'll talk about the claret-colored rug."

Impulsively, Meredith bent down and kissed Annabelle's wrinkled cheek. Then she hurried back down the hall, to the foyer, and the young butler had to run in order to open the front door for her. He looked affronted, and tried to smooth his one stubborn shock of hair.

Outside, Meredith leaned against her van for a moment, then reached for the door handle.

"You were wonderful in there with Annabelle."

Before Meredith could move, Cal's arms had come around her from behind. He kissed the nape of her neck, right there in front of the regimented flowers. She yielded only momentarily to him before she twisted away.

"You have no right, Cal! Especially after that mess you got me into today."

He leaned imperturbably against her van door, preventing her from opening it. "What happened with Cynthia?" he asked. Meredith laughed rather wildly; she couldn't begin to tell him what had happened.

"Let's put it this way," she said. "Cynthia has decided that she can't control me, so I'm out of New Dimensions. She made that very clear."

Cal looked amused. "Not bad for your first day on the job. You managed to win the client over and get fired at the same time."

"That's right. I'm through with New Dimensions. I'd like to go now. Please remove yourself."

"Look, Meredith. You were so good in there with Annabelle. You knew exactly what she needed. I'll have a talk with Cynthia and see if I can't unruffle her feathers. Who knows? Maybe someday you'll be bossing *her* around."

Meredith glared at him. "I can't believe this. You never quit, do you? I don't want to boss anybody around, not even Cynthia Campbell. And I don't want you trying to manage my life anymore!" Her voice trembled with anger and frustration. She gripped the door handle, trying to nudge Cal aside. His body was rock solid, immovable.

Just then Cynthia strode down the walk from the house, moving with easy grace. "I didn't have a chance to say good-bye to you, Meredith,'' she called. ''I do wish you luck.'' She sounded friendly, as if addressing a sorority sister. She positioned herself beside the passenger door of Cal's Jaguar. ''I'm sorry I kept you waiting, Cal,'' she said. ''I'm ready for that lunch you promised me.''

Meredith swallowed, her throat like sandpaper. She waited for Cal to move, staring at his elegant, green tie. Green!

''Cynthia needed a lift this morning,'' Cal muttered to Meredith. ''What did you expect me to do?''

She gave him a long, measuring look. ''I'm sure you really don't want me to answer that.''

''Meredith—''

''She's waiting for you.''

With an oath under his breath, Cal left Meredith. She slipped into the front seat of her van, pulling the door shut and locking it. She watched as Cal opened the door of the Jaguar for Cynthia, saw the way Cynthia's hand lingered for a moment on Cal's arm. Then Cal went around to his own side and the Jaguar swung out of the drive.

Meredith rested her forehead against the steering wheel. She longed for only one thing now—to stop the words echoing in her mind. But they would not go away. They repeated themselves over and over, like a tape recording of Cynthia's cool, mocking voice: *''Why don't you admit you're in love with him? In love with Cal . . .''*

Chapter Ten

Cynthia's question pursued Meredith the rest of the week, until finally she knew she had to stop pussyfooting around and face it head-on. It was a conviction that came to her late Friday afternoon in the produce section of the grocery store. She picked up a bunch of grapes, and asked herself forcefully, almost defiantly, *Am I in love with Cal? Well, am I or not?*

She wanted to discover the truth. Had to know the truth of what was in her own heart. That would be her only strength now.

No answer presented itself in the grapes.

Baffled, Meredith stuffed the grapes into a plastic bag, tossed it into her basket, and pushed on to the lettuce. Maybe the problem was that she didn't know the definition of love. She tried to puzzle it out. Her parents had certainly shared something all these years—her mother would miss Daddy like she would miss her hands or the beat of her own heart. And he'd be like a chicken with its head cut off without her. A strange sort of mutual dependency that her mother called love. And maybe it was, at least for her.

What about Ima Rose? She had believed herself in love with Edward after only five days. Maybe that had been something genuine, too, whether it had lasted for a moment or fifty years. Who could know?

And the way she felt about Cal . . . that was a whole labyrinth of longing and confusion. Who could unravel it?

Meredith sighed and looked down at the head of lettuce she was vigorously squeezing. She pitched it into her basket and headed for the checkout line.

The telephone was ringing when she let herself into the downstairs office portion of her house. She dumped her two bags of groceries on the wet bar counter and grabbed the receiver of the phone on her French provincial desk.

"Grant De—"

"Where have you been?" Cal's voice demanded. "I've been looking all over for you. Don't you ever check your answering machine?"

Meredith frowned, dropped to her desk chair, and began shuffling papers.

"Hello, Cal. If you must know, I had to get my hair cut and then I did my grocery shopping. There was a special on toilet paper."

"How much?" Cal asked, sounding disturbed.

"Four rolls for a dollar. I bought eight. I'd be happy to share, if you need some."

"That wasn't what I meant. How much hair did you get cut off?"

"I have no idea." She brought a strand forward and examined it. "About an inch, I guess. It was only a trim."

"Good. I like your hair long." He barreled onward. "I've been calling all over trying to find you. Kayanne suggested I look in my attic. She says you've been spending a lot of time up there lately. My entire house looks like a tornado just went through it, and meanwhile you start holing up in my attic."

Meredith twirled the telephone cord around her finger. She'd been going up there to search for clues to the story of Ima Rose and Edward. She hoped Cal hadn't noticed all the loose floorboards she'd pried up, looking for a possible cache of love letters.

"And then I phoned your mother," Cal went on.

Meredith pulled on the cord, cutting off the circulation to her finger. "My mother!" she exclaimed. That was all she needed; by now it would be all over Crystal Creek that Meredith had a "feller."

"We had a very enjoyable conversation," Cal said. "She invited both of us for dinner tonight. I'll pick you up at six."

"Not on your life," she declared. "I have no intentions of taking you home to my parents, for dinner or anything else."

"What are you afraid of, Meredith?"

"Nothing. It will be a disaster, that's all. You don't realize what you're getting yourself into. My mother is unpredictible, on a good day, and my dad's worse. Before the evening is over he'll be asking what your intentions are. And he's the sheriff, remember? He carries a gun."

"I'm willing to take the risk. I'm intrigued now. I wouldn't miss this for anything."

Her hand tightened on the receiver. As if he could see her, Cal's voice took on a warning tone. "Don't even think about it, Meredith. You're not going to hang up on me again."

She relaxed her grip only with a great deal of effort, and scowled down at the receiver. "Cal, why was it so urgent for you to talk to me in the first place?"

"I had a meeting with Cynthia today and we settled everything. She still wants you at New Dimensions."

"You've got to be kidding. Cynthia was furious with me over the way I handled Annabelle Mohr."

"As it turns out, Annabelle refuses to work with anyone but you. What do you think about that?"

"I don't know what to think . . . Cal, you have no idea what went on that day between Cynthia and me."

"It doesn't matter. Apparently it's quite a surprise for Annabelle to stand firm like this, and her niece is backing her all the way. This is the time for you to sign with New Dimensions, Meredith. Cynthia will have to agree to your terms—she doesn't have much choice. You can call the shots now, and you accomplished that just by being you. That's really something."

Meredith listened to Cal's voice. It was deep and vibrant, sending currents of warmth over the line. She found herself caught up in that hypnotic current. It seemed she still had a chance to give Kayanne and Bo all the opportunities they deserved. Kayanne had even been making progress with Mrs. Lipscomb; she was developing public relations skills that would make her a success anywhere—even at New Dimensions. Oh, it was tempting to think about proving Cynthia wrong. Meredith fantasized about it. She and Kayanne and Bo sailing into New Dimensions and succeeding magnificently. Nothing ordinary about it. After a while, Cal wouldn't even know Cynthia Campbell was alive.

She put a hand on her desk, trying to ground herself again; nothing seemed clear anymore. Nothing at all. All her moorings were slipping away.

"Are you still there, Meredith?" Cal asked softly.

She cleared her throat. "Yes, I'm here. But I'm not ready for any more pressure from you. Can't you understand that?"

"Actually, that's something else I wanted to talk to

you about.'' He spoke slowly, as if grudging his words. ''Meredith, you've lived up to our deal. In all fairness I can't use it as leverage against you anymore. I gave you the money you needed; you gave New Dimensions a trial. We're even as far as that goes.''

''Well, I'm certainly glad to have that off my back,'' Meredith said fervently. This was indeed cause for celebration. She fished a package of fruit chewy cookies from one of her grocery bags, pulled open the top, and sampled a bite. ''Cal, I do believe you're sounding almost like a reasonable man. Now at least you realize that this is my decision. Not yours. Not Cynthia's. Just mine.''

''It doesn't mean I'm going to stop trying to convince you,'' he said, sounding cantankerous. ''I still think New Dimensions is a big break for you, and I'll do everything I can to make you see that.''

Meredith took another bite of her cookie. ''I'm going to consider New Dimensions very carefully. But I'm not going to make a decision right away.''

''You can't delay too long, Meredith. You won't have this window of opportunity open forever.''

''I'll keep that in mind,'' she said patiently. '' 'Bye, Cal.''

''Don't forget, I'll pick you up at six.'' This time he hung up first, and in quite an abrupt manner. Meredith absently nibbled the rest of her cookie. From now on she was going to be much more frugal with money; anything was better than giving Cal financial power over her. She was free of it now, and she meant to remain free.

That didn't change the fact that she needed to make a decision about New Dimensions. She wanted it to be an intelligent and logical one, but her feelings for Cal kept intruding and confusing her. Worst of all, she wasn't even sure what those feelings were. Love? Despair? Need?

Cal had made life even more complicated by arranging dinner tonight with her parents. He seemed determined to go through with it, though; if he was going to be so stubborn he might as well suffer the consequences.

Hurriedly Meredith took her groceries upstairs and put them away, cramming boxes and cans into the cupboard and shoving everything else haphazardly into the fridge. Next she drew herself a bath in her big old-fashioned, claw-footed tub. A hot bubble bath was always a good therapy technique. Sometime later she emerged from the tub with flushed skin and pruny toes, slightly more resigned to the experience ahead.

Wrapped in a terry-cloth robe, she attacked her closet for something to wear. The red plaid dress? No, that wasn't right at all. The denim dress? White pants and navy tunic top? She could always count on her sapphire-blue dress, of course, but Cal had already seen her in it. . . .

She stopped herself. What was wrong with her, for crying out loud? She was having dinner at her parents' house, not The Mansion. And in Crystal Creek the evening meal was called supper, anyway. And at the Grant house it was usually spelled unadulterated pandemonium. So what was she trying to do, exactly? Sweep Cal off his feet? Ridiculous! She liked to get as much use as possible out of her clothes, regardless of male opinion.

Nevertheless, she rejected the sapphire-blue dress and slipped it back on the hanger, pushing it to the far side of the closet.

At last she pulled out a white peasant blouse and an ankle-brushing skirt of vivid print. She fixed her hair in a thick, glossy braid that hung down her back, applied just a touch of lip gloss, and surveyed herself in the mirror. She looked like a Gypsy. She added gold looped earrings, and impulsively pushed the pouf sleeves off her shoulders.

Cal arrived promptly at six, his arms full of violets. Laughing with delight, Meredith gathered them into her arms.

"Thank you, Cal. You must have bought out an entire shop," she exclaimed as she led the way to her living quarters upstairs.

"Two, as a matter of fact, but who's counting? I remembered you saying that your father always brought violets for your mother." He grinned, the corners of his eyes crinkling. "I don't know about your mother, but violets are a lot like her daughter. They spill out all over everything, and they're beautiful."

Meredith was touched by his words, and lowered her cheek to the violets. Then she busied herself finding vases for them, calling upon some empty jars, as well. She observed her arrangements with satisfaction; violets in old jam jars were pleasing to the eye.

Cal came over to her.

"You arè beautiful, Meredith," he murmured. He lifted his hands to her shoulders, his skin against hers. Without thought or question she raised her face. His mouth captured hers with sweetness, enticing her response. She clung to him as if he were the last stable thing on earth, returning his long and tender kiss. When finally they broke apart, Cal just looked and looked at her. He had very intense, very blue eyes. . . .

With an odd sense of shock, Meredith realized her thoughts were straight from Ima Rose's diary. *He just looked and looked at me. He has very intense, very blue eyes.*

She swallowed. With difficulty.

"If we keep on like this, we'll never make it to your parents'," Cal said wryly. "They are expecting us."

Meredith nodded, and found her handbag. A perfect match for the strappy sandals she was. wearing.

Several cars were parked in the driveway and along the tree-lined curb when they arrived at the Grant house. Meredith wasn't surprised. Cal, on the other hand, looked perplexed.

"What's going on here?" he wanted to know. "It looks like half of Crystal Creek is here."

"Only the half that's kin to me," Meredith said through a deep sigh. As she'd suspected—and knowing her mother—the clan had gathered to meet "Meredith's young man." And it wasn't necessary to be present in order to recite her mother's invitation word for word. "Brace yourself, here comes the first wave," she warned, indicating a group of children running across the yard with a sweep of her hand; they descended like a swarm of locusts. "This is your last chance to escape, Bonner," she added hopefully.

Cal merely shook his head, and forged bravely into the fray.

They gravitated to the backyard with her brothers' and sisters' contribution to the family tree: four boys and a girl belonged to Andy; three girls and a boy were Paul's; two of each for Joleen; several cousins, once or twice removed, and a couple Meredith wasn't sure she recognized.

Roxanne Grant flung the squeaky gate open wide to receive them. She was wearing an oversized tunic top that displayed Mickey Mouse's smiling face, and a pair of baggy shorts. She was barefoot, her hair tied back in a ponytail from which loose tendrils escaped. She handed

Meredith a kitten before kissing her on the cheek. Meredith, the pig, wasn't far behind, leading the parade that included Jo Jo the Lhasa, Sam the Irish setter, Cocoa the Labrador retriever, Happy the spitz, and Sarge the whatever. Meredith wasn't sure whether she was holding Faith, Hope, or Charity. Her mother cuddled the other two kittens, and a large Siamese was draped around her neck.

"Mere! Mr. Bonner!" Roxanne exclaimed. "How wonderful that you could come."

"Please call me Cal."

Roxanne gave him a broad smile. "Come along, then. The burgers are almost ready. Sam is the chef tonight. As Mere can attest, I'm not much of a cook myself, Cal, but her father grills a mean burger, and Joleen fixed her famous potato salad. Oh, dear, I hear Sam calling me. Mere, why don't you introduce your young man around? I'd better see what your father wants." She thrust the two kittens she was holding into Cal's hands.

Meredith rolled her eyes above a severely pained expression. "You asked for this, Bonner," she whispered to Cal out of the corner of her mouth.

Roxanne cleared a path through the animals and children, waving Meredith and Cal into the heart of the loud mix—cousins, aunts and uncles, grannies, in-laws, a few outlaws—not raucous but rich with a tightly woven family tapestry. Brothers and sisters who laughed and teased and all seemed to talk at once. Spouses sailing through the clamor unconcerned. Children cheered by platters of hamburgers and hot dogs and freezers of homemade ice cream. The big yard, shaded by giant pecan trees, was a magnet, ruled over by Sam Grant, whose contribution to the evening festivities was done once the burgers and wieners were grilled. He waved Meredith and Cal into lawn chairs flanking his under one of the big trees. "No, Red, you sit here and talk to me. Your mother doesn't need any help. She and Joleen can handle everything."

Meredith handed her kitten to Meg, Andy's youngest, sat down and smoothed out her skirt, and glanced at Cal. His casual but expensive clothes seemed more suited to dining aboard a corporate jet or yacht. Ralph Lauren and Brooks Brothers were common in Dallas, but Levi's was still the brand of choice in Crystal Creek. Her father was wearing Levi's jeans and a Levi's shirt over the tall, lanky frame that was the mold from which Bo had been made, and a gimme baseball cap advertising motor oil. But Cal leaned back comfortably in the folding lawn chair, a purring kitten perched on each Brooks Brothers-covered knee.

"Tell me about yourself, Cal," Sam Grant said as he bit into the hamburger Roxanne had just handed him on a paper plate. He had an enormous appetite and his wife had provided accordingly. Two burgers, a generous portion of potato salad, baked beans, and a large heap of potato chips on the side. "What do you think of our little town now that you've been here a while? How's your house coming along? How's the newspaper doing these days? What college did you attend? What are your future plans?"

"Well, let's see . . ." Cal answered each question in order, not showing even the slightest annoyance at this interrogation. Meredith frowned down at the paper plate of food her mother had handed her. She was cringing. She actually felt her eyes screw shut, and her mouth make a silent grimace.

The yard was aromatic with the sweetness of lilac bushes and Sam Grant's burgers. The conversation was loud and chaotic. A kind of chain reaction of jokes and

taunts and complaints and broken anecdotes, with shouts
and whoops of laughter booming brassy and shrill above
the general hubbub. Roxanne flitted about happily, at-
tending to everybody's needs.

"Are you ready for another burger, Cal?" Roxanne
asked as she fluttered by to refill Sam's iced tea glass.
Cal said he was. Sam wanted more potato salad. Meredith prodded at her beans with her fork while Cal and
Sam talked.

"So you're not sure whether you're staying in Crystal
Creek or not, huh?" Sam said. "It's a nice place to raise
a family. I wouldn't think of living anywhere else. Red,
here, she's the restless one of our bunch. Pretty as a
picture, but a head full of dreams."

Cal chuckled. "I believe you've pegged her, Mr.
Grant."

"Call me Sam. How do you feel about large families,
Cal? And what about fishing?"

"I'm in favor of both, Sam."

"So why haven't you ever married, Cal?"

"Daddy!"

"I guess the right girl has just . . . never come along."
Cal's gaze roved over Meredith.

"You can't sit around waiting for the right person,"
Sam said through a warm, crinkly smile. "You've got
to go out looking. That's what I keep telling Red. But
you two have done okay for yourself, if I'm any judge."

Color stained Meredith's cheeks. Sam just went on
eating. Cal just sat there looking comfortable in spite of
having to balance two kittens and a paper plate of food,
and with a pig now resting on his expensive Italian loafers. How could he be so at home? He was chatting with
Sam as if they were long-lost cousins. Kindred spirits.
Best buddies! Well, if Cal expected another Roxanne or

Joleen from her he had another thing coming. Her mother and sister were both little girls playing house, and neither had an adult identity. They were obsessed with the role of wife and mother, and in her mother's case, now that her children were grown, she mothered animals. Meredith had never felt as if she truly belonged here. Always she'd been restless, eager to get away and go after her dream and never let it get away.

Roxanne dashed by, chasing a couple of grandkids, the dogs chasing her. A few minutes later she was back, this time with more wild tendrils shooting out from her ponytail, and balancing three bowls of ice cream.

Cal didn't bat an eyelid when the Siamese sprang from around Roxanne's neck onto his lap, missing his ice cream by mere inches. Roxanne waved her arms, nearly swatting Cal.

"Shoo . . . shoo! Where are your manners, Ching Fu?" The seal point darted away, the kittens in pursuit. "If you want any more ice cream," Roxanne said, "just holler. There's plenty." She scurried off again.

Meredith shifted in her chair, and noticed that Kay-anne was saying her good-byes and heading for her car in the drive. Meredith put her half-eaten bowl of ice cream on the ground and came to her feet, barely avoiding stepping on her namesake as the pig flopped over on her side, sighing contentedly, after consuming a couple of burgers herself. "We have to be going now, too," Meredith said. "The burgers were delicious, Daddy, as usual."

"We have plenty of time," Cal countered, settling back more comfortably.

Meredith stared at him. "We have to go right now," she said. "At least I do. If you'd prefer to stay, I'll get Kayanne to take me home."

Cal's mouth twitched, but he came to his feet. "I guess the night is slipping away faster than I thought," he said in a serious tone.

Sam went right on eating his ice cream. But he had watched this exchange with eyes that were altogether too quick and bright.

"I'll go find Mother and say good night," Meredith said.

"Yes, you do that, Red," Sam said. He stood and extended a hand in Cal's direction. "You're welcome here anytime, son."

Cal shook his hand. "I appreciate that, Sam, and I intend to take you up on that offer. Soon."

"See that you do."

Roxanne had no intentions of settling for a mere handshake; she kissed Cal on both cheeks and then hugged him for good measure. He didn't mention the baby rabbit that was nestled in Roxanne's hair, and neither did Meredith.

She headed for the car, but Cal placed a hand on her arm. "Let's take a walk after all that food. What do you say?"

"Fine." She turned and went in the other direction. "Don't tell me you're complaining about my father's burgers," she threw over her shoulder.

"Of course not." He kept pace with her easily. "I always enjoy a walk after a good meal."

"Well, that's fine. Just peachy keen." She lengthened her stride, but Cal barely had to accelerate.

Several of the neighborhood kids were playing baseball under the streetlights; rock music blared from a car parked down the street. All the houses streamed light. Cookie-cutter houses that might have been a stage set for "The Andy Griffith Show." Mayberry, U.S.A.

"You know," Cal remarked, "any other woman might be happy for a man to like her parents."

"I'm glad you like them. The three of you should set up shop together."

"What's wrong, Red?"

"Nothing—and don't call me that!"

He shrugged mildly. They went on walking. The silence between them was covered by the rock music and by the shouts of children. At the corner Meredith turned back.

"I just want to go home," she said.

"They're not so bad, you know. I see a lot of you in your mother, as a matter of fact."

Meredith pulled herself up short. "Mother and I are nothing alike!"

"Yes, you are, Meredith. Whether you want to admit it or not, you are."

"And I suppose one dinner makes you an expert on the subject, does it? You think you can just waltz into my life and sum it all up!"

"I'm fair at a waltz, and I've rebelled against my own parents, just like everybody else. It goes with the territory."

"Oh, wonderful!" Meredith went on walking. "Chalk it up to a little rebellion left over from my teens. Didn't you see how she waits on my father hand and foot? They remind me of Edith and Archie Bunker. My mother never aspired to anything except to be a wife and mother, and lately a zookeeper." At last Meredith understood something. She looked up at Cal. "Don't you see?" she asked. "My father is the controlling type, but he's not the one stopping her. It's her. She's the one responsible for wasting her own life and talents. No one but her."

This fact was so basic, so utterly simple, that she

didn't know why she'd never realized it before. She had always blamed her father for holding Roxanne back, preventing her from being something other than his wife and the mother of his children. The truth was that her mother had created her own life, molded it to her own satisfaction, just as Joleen was doing.

Cal was gazing down at Meredith in the pool of light cast by a street lamp.

"I think you're being too hard on both your parents," he said. "I've never met a happier woman than your mother. I don't know if you're aware of it or not, but steam practically comes off her when she's with your father and he with her, and they touch each other a lot. Everybody should be so lucky to have that."

Meredith stood very still. "Cal, I'm way ahead of you on this," she said. "Tonight I've really seen my parents the way they actually are together, not how I always imagined them. You're right, my mother couldn't be happier. Daddy's her knight in shining armor, and what they have works for them." She felt she had taken a step into the future—her own future, not a repetition of the life her parents had. But that was more frightening than anything she'd ever done before. Without those hang-ups to cloud her vision, she could see Cal so clearly now. She could see herself, and the way she felt about him.

She wasn't ready, after all! Not for this. Not for the stark, elemental knowledge that she loved Cal. She made a desperate struggle against it.

"Please, take me home," she said. She went to the Jaguar. Cal caught hold of her arm.

"What is it, Meredith? The look on your face just now. What's wrong?" He was being gentle. Oh, why did he have to be such a wonderful, endearing mixture of tenderness and stubbornness, idealism and hard practicality?

"Don't ask me any more questions, Cal," she begged. "Just take me home."

He obliged her this time, and they maintained a strained silence during the drive. When he pulled up in front of her house, she wouldn't let him come inside, or even walk her to the door.

She shut her front door and locked it with shaking hands, then ran up the stairs. She looked around at the profusion of violets. And she knew she couldn't lock Cal out of her heart or her mind.

She loved him. She was deeply and irrevocably in love with Cal Bonner.

Chapter Eleven

"Hi ya, Doc," Meredith said as she approached her grandfather, who was fishing at the eastern edge of Crystal Creek, a good twelve miles from where the body of water began its meandering in the town that bore its name. A spot that was invisible to a casual observer, for huge growths of sunflowers and mesquite bushes hid it until, when you were right up to it, you saw the gap, and the worn earth of a path between the sunflowers. This was where Joe Snider could be found every morning between six and nine A.M.

"Well, if it isn't my favorite granddaughter," he said, squinting up at Meredith through a glare of sunlight. "What brings you out here to the sticks on such a hot morning, girl?" His laughter rang out. It was infectious, and Meredith smiled back weakly. "Sit, sit!" The hand not holding the fishing pole was scratching the head of a large golden retreiver named Bingo, who accompanied him everywhere. The dog was old. His large tongue lolled out and he panted loudly.

Doc was seventy-three, but he wasn't old. He was a retired veterinarian and part-time farmer, and everybody called him "Doc." He was a massive man, heavy through the shoulders and belly, with arms and legs like the trunks of small trees and hands so large it seemed impossible that they could be as gentle as they were. He wore faded overalls, an old chambray shirt, and a battered straw hat that looked as if he might have inherited it from *his* grandfather. Altogether an essentially sloppy man who liked animals even more than his daughter, Roxanne.

Joining him on the sandy bank, Meredith said, ''I came by to see you, Doc. What else? Catching any fish?'' She tried on a smile that didn't seem to fit quite right.

Doc noticed that, too. ''What's wrong with you, girl? If you don't mind my saying so, you look like something the dogs drug up and the cats wouldn't eat.''

''I guess it's the heat,'' she lied. She hadn't slept at all last night, not after the revelation of her love. She couldn't confide this to anyone, not even Doc, and least of all Cal. He was attracted to her; she was sure about that much. But that didn't mean he would ever love her.

She didn't want to love him! She wanted her old, carefree self back. She'd been so happy and independent before she met him. What was going to happen to her now?

''Nice day for wool gathering,'' Doc said, breaking through her thoughts. His eyes were small and very bright blue and nearly buried in a network of fine crinkles, as if he laughed a great deal, which he did. His shaggy eyebrows were, like his head and chest hair, the red of rusted steel, with gray under it. He was all over freckles, freckles so dense they ran together across the bridge of his nose, as if he were wearing a copper mask. There were freckles on his hands and arms, too. His hair, once curly, was now merely frizzled, and looked as if it had been combed with an egg beater, if combed at all. The blue chips of his eyes took in Meredith with good humor and even sympathy. ''Come on, girl,'' he said.

"Something's troubling you. Has it got anything to do with that nice young man Roxanne had us all over to meet last night and Sam was giving the third degree?"

"No," she said. But she didn't sound very convincing. Two lies in less than a minute. Must be some sort of record. She could almost feel her nose growing longer. She gave Bingo an affectionate scratch behind the ears, earning a major wag of his tail. Abundant spoor announced that deer, bobcats, squirrels, rabbits, coyotes, and other wildlife visited this part of the creek regularly to drink from the cool, clear water. Cattle grazed on rolling hills to the north; there were strings of horses under shade trees. The green roof of her grandparents' prairie-style house poked up between the cottonwood trees that grew along the banks of the creek. "Actually," Meredith said at last, "I'm here to pick your brains, Doc, or at least I hope you can help me. I was wondering, did your father talk much about the time he spent at Camp Sam Houston?"

"Some. But what in the Sam Hill made you think of that?" He poked around in his pockets until he produced a packet of red licorice. "Want some?"

"Sure." She told him about the diary she'd found in the attic of the House of the Seasons. Doc chuckled in his deep bass.

"That would be Edward Bumgardner," he said. "Miss Ima's husband."

"Husband?" Meredith looked at him and blinked, completely baffled. "Doc, I think you've been out in the sun too long. Ima Rose died a spinster."

"What gave you that idea? Oh, wait a minute. It's the name. That confuses lots of folks. Maybe I should back up, begin at the beginning, and I remember it all like it was yesterday, although I was only six years old at the time.

"Captain Bumgardner was a handsome devil. My mother wasn't too keen on him, though. You see, he and my daddy had become good friends over there at the camp, and Daddy would bring him home to supper once in a while. He was single, and quite the gay blade, and Mama was sure he'd lead Daddy down the path of ruin. Mama and Ima Rose were best friends during their school days, and she didn't think the captain was Ima Rose's type. Nobody did. But Ima Rose wasn't any angel. She was a young woman ahead of her time. A regular rabble rouser, as it turned out."

"What do you mean?" Meredith asked, chewing thoughtfully on her licorice.

"She was into all that women's suffrage stuff and took on some of the biggest union bosses in Big D for good measure. . . . But I'm getting ahead of myself. It was no secret in Crystal Creek that Ima Rose and Captain Bumgardner were carrying on. But you know how that is. Somebody around here sneezes and half the town says God bless you. Anyway, after the captain shipped out, Ima Rose just up and disappeared. I guess you could say she ran away from home. Old man Benjamine hired a detective to find her, and he did, over in Dallas. She was just a kid, but somehow she'd finagled her way into a job at the *Globe*. Nothing to write home about at first. Just on the city desk, but anybody who knew Ima Rose knew she wouldn't stay there long, and she didn't. I don't know what went on between her and old man Benjamine, but Ima Rose didn't come home, and when she wasn't marching and speaking out for the ratification of the Nineteenth Amendment, she was exposing corruption in unions." Doc laughed again. "My daddy was fit to

be tied when Mama joined in on several of those suffra-
gette rallies. Mama didn't pay him a bit of mind, though;
she'd just load up our Model T with a bunch of her
friends and hightail it over to Big D. I figure you got
your spirit from her, girl.

"Anyway, Edward did make it back from the Great
War, and he and Ima Rose were married. But she kept
her maiden name for professional reasons—all her read-
ers knew her as Ima Rose Benjamine. Her column was
syndicated across the country at one time." Doc
searched methodically through his pockets again. Some
were so small only a thumb could poke inside them;
others held pencils, fishing lures, a Swiss army knife, a
New Testament. At last he pulled out a bag of ginger-
snaps. He handed one to Meredith, another to Bingo, and
munched on one himself. He had apple juice in one ther-
mos, water in another. Meredith and Doc had the juice.
Bingo lapped water from the bowl Doc had brought
along.

"I don't know for sure what kind of marriage those
two had," he said to Meredith. "Ima Rose worked at
the newspaper and wrote several books. The only one I
can remember was called *The Long and Winding Road.*
It was about women's rights, naturally. My mama had a
copy, much to Daddy's eternal chagrin. He didn't have
the nerve to burn it, though. The captain traveled with a
flying show for a while. He was known as Daredevil
Bumgardner, Ace of the Skies. He was killed in a plane
crash. Must have been somewhere around 1929 or '30.
That's when Ima Rose returned to Crystal Creek. Her
daddy was ailing by then, and Ima cared for him and her
mama until their deaths. She never had any children of
her own, but she always had a flock of kids about her.
Neighborhood kids like me. She made the best fudge

I've ever tasted. And I reckon that's about it, girl. All us kids called her Miss Ima, and I suppose that's why you assumed she was a spinster.''

Meredith gave a slow, deep sigh. The story of Ima Rose and Edward was now complete for her. They had loved each other. But that thought evoked a much more recent memory, a magical moment in a stuffy attic. Bingo's eyes were closing. Meredith blinked, tears stinging her eyes. She struggled to her feet. Bingo opened his eyes and looked at her in annoyance.

''I guess I'd better be going, Doc. Thanks for the information.''

''You look tired, girl. Why don't you come up to the house with me? Your grandmother was just putting one of her German chocolate cakes in the oven when I left. It should be done and iced by now. A big slice of that with a tall glass of cold milk would hit the spot right now. What do you say?''

''I'd love to, Doc, but I am a working girl.''

''On Saturday?''

Meredith laughed. ''Look who's talking. You use to work seven days a week, twenty-four hours a day.'' She leaned over and kissed his freckled cheek and patted Bingo's head. ''Give Nanna my love, and I'll see you both real soon.''

''Take another gingersnap for the road. And bring your young man next time.''

She munched on the gingersnap, blinking furiously, as she hurried to the winding dirt road that skirted the creek where she'd left her van. Dallas or Cal's? She put the van in gear and headed for town. She drove straight through, foot to the accelerator.

It wasn't any use. She felt as if she were bound to Cal by invisible cords, tugging her toward him. She passed the entrance ramp to Highway 20, took a right at the next intersection, circled back until she came to Fillmore Street, and pulled into the drive behind the Jaguar. Emerging slowly from her van, she stood against it for a moment. Then she gripped her briefcase and strode up the walk.

Cal was wearing jeans and had his feet propped up on the coffee table in the library. Meredith stared at his blue-and-yellow checkered socks.

"Hi," she said softly. He lowered the newspaper he'd been reading and sat up straight.

"Hi yourself."

"Um, I guess I'll just get to work. . . ."

"Sit down, Meredith. Let's talk," he urged. She balanced herself uneasily on the edge of an armchair and gazed at him. Why did he have to look so devastatingly handsome? Long-muscled and slender, and tanned, probably from tennis. He had never mentioned playing the game, but that was a favorite pastime of the rich and famous, wasn't it? Cynthia looked like the tennis type, too.

For a while neither of them said anything. Meredith looked at the smear of paint on the sleeve of Cal's shirt; she wondered if he even knew it was there. It was cornflower blue, the same shade as the trim in one of the upstairs bathrooms.

"So, Cal," she began at last, "have you made up your mind yet? About what you're going to do next, I mean. San Francisco? France? Or buy the *Chronicle* and go independent?"

"I haven't decided." He smiled at her. "I'm procrastinating, just the way you are. Maybe we're more alike than I thought."

"Maybe we feel the same way . . . about a few things."

"Do you like Humphrey Bogart movies?" Cal asked.

"Yes," she admitted.

"What about organ music at baseball games, and hot dogs?"

"Who doesn't?"

"So there you have it. Already we agree on two major issues. We can always compromise on the rest."

"Cal, there's only one issue that matters," Meredith burst out.

"What's that?" he asked with interest.

She sprang up, afraid that she really would tell him. Say out loud that any compromise could be reached—if only he loved her. No way was she going to let herself say it. Being in love with Cal was like being swept away by a tidal wave. She actually felt she would give up anything—even her independence—to win his love. How could she have allowed this to happen?

She headed for the door like a drowning victim making one last desperate swim toward land.

"Wait," Cal said. "I want to hear about it. What do you think is the most important issue, Meredith?"

"I'm busy," she answered with determination. "I'm going upstairs to work."

"You don't need to work right now."

"Yes, I do."

The phone jangled sharply from the hall. They both made a dash for it, but Meredith got there first.

"Hello!"

"Mere, it's Kayanne. Guess what! I've just made a major breakthrough with Mrs. Lipscomb. She invited me to have lunch at her house today, and we sat on chairs. Real chairs!"

"That's nice," Meredith said distractedly. Cal was leaning against the wall next to her, his fingers tracing a path down her cheek.

"I don't think you understand the significance of this, Mere," Kayanne said, her voice squeaking with excitement. "We've reached an agreement! We've decided that two of her rooms will have a Japanese motif—cushions, short tables, the works. But the rest of the house stays with the French antiques all the way!"

Meredith made an effort to concentrate. Cal's fingers had found an extremely sensitive spot behind her ear. "Kayanne, that is . . . wonderful news. I . . . I knew you'd handle everything . . . superbly. Does this mean we can finally—" Cal's lips were feathering her left eyebrow. She closed her eyes.

"What's that, Mere?"

"Um . . . can we expect payment—"

"She promised to write out a check first thing Monday morning."

"That's great, Kayanne," Meredith murmured. "That's just wonderful . . . but I really have to go now. I'll talk to you later." She hung up the phone blindly, and rested her forehead on Cal's chest. He massaged her shoulders.

"You're all tense," he said. "Relax. Does that feel good?"

"Oh, yes." His touch was all she craved right now.

"Meredith, I talked to Cynthia again today. She says that New Dimensions will let you keep the Grant Designs name."

Meredith opened her eyes and stared at the blue strips of his shirt. How could he be talking about New Dimensions? Couldn't he tell what was happening to her? It was a cataclysm of her entire being. It was a tempest, and he was at the very center of it. Yet he didn't even know.

"That's not all Cynthia agreed to," he went on. "She's promised that none of your client consultations will be supervised—not even the ones with Annabelle and her niece." He rubbed Meredith's shoulders some more. "Loosen up, you're tensing your muscles."

She pulled away from him.

"You picked your moment again, didn't you?" she accused. "You waited until you thought you had me all happy and relaxed, and then you started in about New Dimensions!"

"For pity sakes, Meredith, I'm just trying to negotiate a good deal for you. Cynthia is cooperating a lot more than you are. That's pretty ironic, when you think about it. She's being professional. Why can't you do the same?"

Suddenly the decision seemed very simple. Meredith wanted to fight Cynthia; she *needed* to fight! Loving Cal was something she could never escape. Okay, that was settled. She wouldn't run away anymore. Instead, she would confront Cynthia and go to battle for Cal. New Dimensions would be the battleground.

A small part of her tried to protest, clamoring that this was not the way to make a business decision. She would be using New Dimensions for her own private ends then—just like Cynthia.

The protest was swept away by a wave of exhilaration. She had a plan of action now and she needed that more than anything else.

"I'll do it," she said, looking directly at Cal. "That's right, I'm going to join New Dimensions."

* * *

Everything was arranged quickly and smoothly. Before Meredith was ready for it, the big morning arrived. Today she was going to sign a contract with New Dimensions.

She woke with a sense of dread that would not go away. Reminding herself that she was joining New Dimensions for one important reason—to fight for Cal—she resolutely got out of bed and slipped into the new dress she had bought for the occasion, to give her fortitude and confidence. It was a swirl of amber silk. The material was soft, cool, and soothing as it settled against her skin. She turned in front of the mirror.

The dress was cut in elegant simplicity, with cap sleeves and a V neck and softly belted waist. The color brought out the gold in her hair and the rose of her complexion.

Meredith looked at the price tag that was still attached to one of the sleeves, and winced. She had been so careful with money lately, determined that never again would she suffer financial bondage to Cal. The dress was not part of her new budget. Of course, once she was working for New Dimensions she'd probably be able to afford ten dresses like this. The idea didn't cheer her at all.

What was she getting herself into today? All the money in the world couldn't replace her freedom.

She sighed. Heavily. She couldn't think about that now or her resolve would truly waver.

She was ready in the amber dress when Cal picked her up at her house later in the morning. At first they were tense with each other. But once they were standing in front of the New Dimensions building, Cal took Meredith's hand and drew her close.

''You're luminous,'' he said. ''You shine with your own light.'' His fingers brushed through the flaming curls of her hair. Then he released her gently. "You're going to dazzle them, Red." Ever since she'd announced her decision to him, he had been so excited for her, so proud of her. And she basked in his approval. She was even willing to overlook him calling her Red.

She walked with him toward the plate-glass doors and her reflection bounced back at her, distorted. She paused, taking a gulp of air. She *was* doing the right thing. Surely, surely she was doing the right thing. She didn't have time to ponder any doubts. Her decision to join New Dimensions had gained a momentum all its own. Now it propelled her forward to the elevator and up to the flamingo-pink world of Cynthia Campbell.

"Hello, Cal, Meredith. I'm pleased we're going to work together, after all." Cynthia was cool and businesslike today. She wore a severe black dress, which heightened her dramatic beauty. Meredith would not let this intimidate her; she looked her best today. She regarded Cynthia steadily, and Cynthia finally gave a faint smile.

"You've managed to drive quite a bargain for Grant Designs, Meredith. I have to congratulate you on that. Along with everything else, you're getting one of the best offices on the floor. Right across from mine, in fact."

And right where you can keep an eye on me, Meredith thought. It hadn't been possible to win a concession on all points. The fight, however, had barely started; Meredith didn't expect or even want it to be easy. Her success at New Dimensions would be all the more triumphant if it was hard-earned. She went with Cal into Cynthia's office.

"Cal, are you sure you finally approve of the contract?" Cynthia asked in a teasing voice, all her attention on him now. "You're more thorough than most lawyers I know."

"I wanted Meredith to have the best deal possible," he said mildly. "And I've had an attorney look it over—Meredith's brother, Paul."

"Why, don't you trust me?" Cynthia said, feigning offense.

Cal shrugged and said, "I'll let Meredith read over the contract for herself now. Go ahead, Meredith. Take your time."

Cynthia made an impatient gesture, but Meredith sat down and read each clause carefully and thoroughly. She had no doubts that she would find everything in order, especially since Paul was involved; she just needed to delay signing her name for a few more moments. It gave her the illusion that her life was still normal, still her own.

At last she had to raise her head and nod her acceptance. She picked up a pen and inched it toward the signature line. Cynthia's low, throaty voice took over.

"I'm glad we'll have this out of the way now, Meredith. Everything is set up for you to meet with Annabelle and Cecy tomorrow, which means we have a lot to accomplish today. Your schedule is typed out for you right here. You'll go to Personnel for briefing, then you'll meet with another client.

"I'll give you his folder and I'll expect you to know the contents. I won't be standing over you, but I certainly don't want any more slip-ups with our clients."

Meredith's pen hovered over the contract. Cynthia's voice went on relentlessly. "You'll have appointments this afternoon with two of our vice-presidents. Just look interested no matter how much they drone on—we try to keep them as happy as possible. And at seven you'll

meet with Susan McKinny for dinner. She's very influential upstairs, Meredith, so of course you'll wear something . . . suitable.''

The pen froze on the signature line. Meredith took a
deep, cleansing breath and set the pen down.

After listening to Cynthia, she understood. If she
signed her name on this contract, every day of her life
she'd be fighting with Cynthia over petty details, over
bits and pieces of time and expenses typed up on a sheet
of paper. That's how it would be. Not a grand and glo-
rious struggle to win Cal's love.

''Is something wrong?'' Cynthia asked politely. Meredith looked at her and saw the brittle wariness under-
neath Cynthia's beauty. Then Meredith looked at Cal.
His face was carefully expressionless, but he returned
her gaze intently. She gave a little shrug.

''I need some time to think,'' she said. She ignored
Cynthia's grimace of frustration, sat back in her chair,
and clasped her hands in her lap. She thought deeply
about the reasons she had decided to join New Dimensions. She had needed so badly to prove something to
Cal, to show him that she could triumph in Cynthia's
world. Perhaps she could . . . but she didn't want that
kind of success. It would mean compromising the person
she really was. And no matter how much she loved Cal,
she could not do that.

Meredith stood up. If Cal was ever going to love her
at all, it would have to be for herself. She didn't belong
to Cynthia's world, and could no longer pretend that she
did. That was not a declaration of independence from
Cal. It was simply a calm, strong ability to look inside
herself and know what was right for her. She felt that
today, for the first time, she had a glimpse of true independence. It was an action, not a reaction.

''I've changed my mind,'' she said. ''You can't have Grant Designs.''

Cynthia's face went cold and hard. ''We've bent over backward to accommodate you, Meredith. I'm sure you realize that.''

''I do, and I'm genuinely sorry to have wasted so much of your time.'' She made a move toward the door.

''Wait a minute!'' Cynthia snapped. ''You're not going to do this to me, Meredith. I've practically kissed the floor for old Annabelle because of you!''

''I believe you saw a little profit in it for yourself,'' Meredith said, still calm. ''Good day, Cynthia.''

''I'll sue you for this!''

''Cal can give you my lawyer's address and telephone number.''

''Cal, you'd better do something—''

''Sorry, Cynthia. She has a mind of her own.'' Cal took Meredith's elbow and ushered her to the elevator. The doors glided shut noiselessly and Cynthia's outraged face disappeared.

Meredith stared at a flamingo-covered wall. ''I know what you must be thinking, Cal. I know how much you disapprove of me right now. But I guess that's just the way it has to be.''

Without quite knowing how it happened, she found herself engulfed in his arms. He chuckled. ''I'm proud of you, Meredith Grant.''

''You are?''

''You bet I am. I still think you have the worst work and business habits known to mankind—or womankind for that matter. But you sure know how to make an exit.''

''Cal . . .'' she whispered against his chest, closing her eyes. She reveled in the feel of his arms.

"I didn't mean to railroad you, Meredith. When you walked out of there, I realized I'd been pushing you too hard."

"I just wanted to make you . . . like me," she murmured. "That's not exactly the best way to conduct business."

"Meredith, don't you realize by now it doesn't matter what you do? You could paint my entire house flamingo pink and I still wouldn't be able to resist you."

"Oh, Cal—" She couldn't finish, because his mouth had captured hers. He kissed her thoroughly, holding her tight. It really was possible to be her own independent self and still have Cal close to her.

The elevator doors slid open. Meredith and Cal slowly disentangled. She was in a delicious daze.

"Good morning!" Cal called out cheerfully to several amused faces. "Wonderful day, isn't it?"

Meredith smoothed her hair back from her flushed cheeks. Cal put his arm around her and propelled her out of the building. "I really didn't mean to force you into anything with New Dimensions," he said. "It just seemed like such a good idea to me. And you did take the place by storm."

"Well, I have been thinking about some of your other ideas, Cal," she said solemnly. "And you're right. Unless I get control of my finances I could lose the freedom my business gives me. I don't want that to happen, and I want to offer Kayanne and Bo something more, too. The first thing I'm going to do is hire an accountant."

"Great! That's a very sound move, Meredith. I'll get the names of some good accounting firms for you—"

"Hold on, financial adviser. That's it for today."

"All right," he said, conceding. "This is your day, Red. Your celebration. Where to?"

There were so many possibilities. It didn't matter which one she chose as long as she was with Cal.

She finally decided on Canton, for First Monday Trade Days, which was the nation's largest flea market. A three-hundred-acre hodgepodge of who-knows-what-you'll-see-next that was to browsers what a marathon was to a distance runner. Placed end to end, the zigzagging rows of tables, tents, and booths chock full of stuff would stretch thirty miles. The otherwise tranquil East Texas town of just over 2,000 was an hour's drive east of Dallas.

Meredith and Cal wandered past stalls of hand-me-down glassware, trophies, knives, guitars, military uniforms, wagon wheels, clocks, and glossies of Humphrey Bogart that were strewn on folding tables. A rusty red scooter caught Meredith's eye; the price sounded too high and she asked for a lower one, and got it. "Dickering is part of the deal," she said. There were vintage jukeboxes, pinball machines, and other coin-operated amusements. They bought corn dogs, dipped them in mustard, and drank lemonade. Cal gave her a kiss; his lips tasted of lemon and mustard. Together they selected a watercolor for the house—sailboats on a lake.

"For the library," Cal said.

"You're reading my mind." Meredith smiled up at him and got another kiss. Hands clasped, they strolled past more stalls. "Books," Meredith said, spying a large tent and dragging Cal toward it. "That's what we need, books. Lots and lots of books for all those shelves in the library." Inside, she introduced him to the art of dusting off book covers and carefully opening cracked bindings of nineteenth-century books.

"I used to love *Black Beauty*," she said. "And look— *Gulliver's Travels*, and here's *Jane Eyre*. Here's an author I've never heard of before, but I think we should take all his books. He was very prolific. I like that.''

The vendor, a man wearing a red bandanna and a beaded necklace, loaned Meredith a big apron to protect her dress as she went squeezing among the grimy shelves. Her pile of books grew to a respectable size, but so far Cal had only decided on one mystery novel. Meredith shook her head in disapproval.

''That's not how you shop for books, Cal. You have to get into the spirit of things.''

''I made that mistake the last time I went shopping with you,'' he said grimly. He chose one more mystery as his contribution, and watched with a pained expression as the backseat and trunk of the Jaguar filled up with books.

''I love the smell of musty pages,'' Meredith declared. ''It promises all those long, satisfying hours of reading. There's nothing quite like it.''

Cal coughed and rolled down the window. ''Nothing like it,'' he agreed dryly. They headed for Crystal Creek, then carried all the books inside Cal's house and stacked them wherever they could find an empty space. Meredith was glad she and Cal had the house to themselves. She balanced a copy of *Grimm's Fairy Tales* on the library mantel. But today she didn't need any fairy tales. She had her own life. Her own love.

She turned and found Cal watching her from the doorway. He gave her a wide-eyed look suggestive of passion that she responded to in kind. She hesitated only a moment, then walked toward him.

He caught her close, burying his face in her hair. ''Meredith, maybe I'd better leave right now. I've never seen you look so desirable,'' he murmured huskily.

''This is your house, remember?'' she whispered

against his neck. She lifted her head and claimed his mouth for her own. His hands moved down the length of her back, caressing her through the silk.

His kisses grew more demanding, more urgent. Hands twining through the masses of her hair, he arched her face back to his.

"Meredith . . ." His breath was as ragged as hers, his eyes dark as he gazed down at her. She clung to him, burying her face in his neck. Their hearts beat wildly together. "You're so beautiful," he murmured thickly, his fingers brushing over the smooth, creamy skin of her throat, but still he wasn't close enough.

"Cal, I love you so much!" The words were out before she could stop them. His hands on her tensed. "Cal?" she whispered.

"Come away with me, Meredith," he said roughly. "Tonight. Tomorrow. Just come away with me."

She buried her head against his shoulder so that he couldn't see her face. "What do you mean?"

"We can go anywhere you like. I don't know what will happen. We can take it one day at a time."

"What will we be? Friends? Lovers?" The words caught in her throat. She closed her eyes tightly.

"I don't know . . . both. Isn't that enough? Neither of us needs anything more right now."

"I need more, Cal," she cried from the depths of her heart.

He was silent. She clung to him, willing him to say the words she longed so desperately to hear. Willing him to say he loved her. To make that commitment to her.

"I want you so much, Meredith."

She closed her eyes even tighter. With one heaving effort she pulled away from him.

"Meredith, what's wrong?" He was beside her in an instant, reaching his hands out to her.

"No!" She twisted away from him and backed toward the door, hugging her arms to her chest. He stared back at her, his face expressionless. Even in the mellow afternoon light the angles of his jaw and cheekbones were sharpened. He looked harsh and uncompromising.

Meredith whirled and stumbled through the hall, out the front door. She looked around frantically for her van, then remembered Cal had picked her up today. She ran all the way to her parents' house, turning to gaze back once. Cal hadn't followed her.

She asked to borrow her mother's car. For once Roxanne didn't ask any questions.

Later that night Meredith huddled in her bed. She was shivering as if in the throes of a fever. On the bedside table she had propped up the photograph of herself and Cal—locked together in an embrace and yet fighting each other so stubbornly. She stared at the photograph, waiting for the telephone to ring. The hours passed in silence.

At last she wept, cradling her forehead on her knees. But her wracking sobs were no comfort, gave no easing of the deep pain inside her heart.

Chapter Twelve

The House of the Seasons was finished, and Meredith walked through it one last time. The new decor included designer wallpaper, ceiling fans, and updated baths. Most of the rooms featured built-ins, Pella doors and windows, and plantation shutters. The hardwood floors were all refinished. Throughout there was a combined sense of openness and light.

The morning room was cheerful and airy, the Shaker table and two matching chairs that she and Cal had purchased together sitting in front of the rounded wall of windows that gave you the feeling of being outdoors. The white-and-teal kitchen had a European tile backsplash and Corian countertops. Everything was arranged so Cal could cook omelets with ease.

She quickened her pace as she went out to the hall. In a corner was a magnificent old grandfather clock. She had searched all over for it, making sure it chimed loudly every fifteen minutes. She hurried past it, going up the stairs.

The master suite, done in shades of hunter green and wine, overlooked perennials and azaleas that had been planted in the garden. There was a sitting area with a wood-burning fireplace and walk-in closets . . . and here was the Shaker bureau she and Cal had picked out together.

Down the hall was the study she'd created for Cal. The furniture was burnished cherrywood, the carpet a warm, muted scarlet. Floor-to-ceiling shelves had been installed; they held some of the books she and Cal also purchased together. Everywhere she turned there were memories. Across the hall was the room where the Caylor print hung in a place of honor. She had built the entire room around it, using heavy pine furniture and subtle shades of chocolate and beige for a rustic look that exuded an Old West ambience.

She walked slowly back down the stairs to the library. This room, in tones of burnt orange and earthy brown, was the most inviting of all. The wainscoting was finished at last, the shelves stocked with the rest of those musty old books. The decrepit sofa had managed to retain its place, but looked jaunty in new upholstery. Above it was displayed the sailboat watercolor she and Cal had purchased at Canton.

Everything should have been perfect. Meredith had created a warm, homey atmosphere throughout the house. It was the sort of place where children should pound up and down the stairs, dogs should pad through the hall, a husband and wife should kiss hello and good-bye at the front door. Her house, with the frescoes in the dome, the cupola, the tall arched windows and bracketed cornices. Only it wasn't her house. It never really had been.

She thought about Ima Rose returning here as a widow, to care for her aging parents, and wondered if this house had ever been a happy place. Ima Rose and her Edward never kissed hello or good-bye at the front door, never shared a moment together here. Meredith thought that was horribly sad. Or perhaps the ache in her heart had merely engulfed her. The unbelievable ache of knowing Cal didn't love her.

She hadn't seen him at all since that disastrous afternoon, for he was never at the house anymore. His silence was terrible proof that she'd done the right thing that day. If he cared for her at all then surely he would not have disappeared so completely, so abruptly from her life.

She had picked up the telephone to call him a dozen times during the past few days. She had dialed the newspaper once. Ellen said Cal was out of town and she had no idea when he would return. Which was just as well. Meredith didn't know what she would have said to him, anyway.

That last afternoon with him haunted her. What had it really meant to him? What if she'd stayed?

A wave of desolation swept over her, so intense that she pressed her hand to her stomach. If only Cal loved her. If only . . .

She fled the house and went straight to Annabelle Mohr's Dallas mansion. Meredith was grateful that she'd been invited for tea; she was seeking any refuge she could find. Today Annabelle's dark, cluttered rooms offered solace, a retreat from color and life—and therefore a retreat from pain.

Annabelle served the tea from an elaborate silver service. There were bite-sized sandwiches with the crusts removed, miniature pastries dusted in powdered sugar, cookies in shapes of stars, slivers of pound cake. Arranging a suitable assortment on the plates under Annabelle's supervision took a while. Meredith found herself soothed by the prolonged ritual. For a moment she could believe that taking tea properly was her only problem in the world.

"There now." Annabelle seemed satisfied at last and sat back. "I just wanted to chat today, Meredith—may I call you Meredith? But I must confess that I also have business motives. I still want you to be my interior decorator."

Meredith smiled wonderingly over her teacup. "Even after the upset with New Dimensions?"

"Most definitely." Annabelle took a minute bite of pastry, patted her lips with a linen napkin, and went on. "I enjoyed that thoroughly, you know. Cecy was in fits."

"I'm sorry—"

"No apologies needed." She waved her hand. "I haven't felt so energetic in years. You will take me on, won't you?"

"Only as a friend. I'll be happy to advise you on your house, and we'll work on it a bit at a time."

"I will pay you exactly what you charge everyone else, and there's an end to it. You'll come to tea again," Annabelle went on happily, "and you'll bring that nice young man, Mr. Bonner."

Meredith set her cup down with a little clatter. "I don't believe so," she stumbled, trying futilely to recover herself. Annabelle set down her own cup.

"Dear me, how foolish of me. I didn't realize. Is it very serious, Meredith?"

"Yes." The word came out involuntarily. She concentrated on a sugar cookie.

"Does he know?"

"He must."

"Dear me."

They were silent. Annabelle stirred her tea thoughtfully, then spoke again. "I want to tell you something about the man who built this house, Meredith. Hamlet

Mohr, my grandfather. He was from a banking family and made it big in the oil field. He left his two children, my father and uncle, hundreds of of millions. Before he died he controlled over a hundred companies ranging in everything from insurance to publishing. He told his sons that money is a lot like manure. Pile it all in one place and it stinks like heck. Spread it around and it does a lot of good. And spread it around he did, the manure and the money. He was a rascal, my grandfather, but he knew how to live. He knew how to face his fears head-on, even when he was a very old man. I should have been like him, I worshiped him so much. But I was a very timid, very uncertain young girl, Meredith. I wasn't brave like my grandfather. Still . . . I fell in love. That should have given me some courage.''

''And it didn't?'' Meredith asked softly.

Annabelle shook her head until her gray ringlets quivered.

''No. And yet I believe he could have loved me. I believe there was a possibility there, if I had known how to grasp it.''

''What if you're ready to take the chance, and he's not?''

''I don't know what to tell you, my dear. I'm certainly not one who should give advice. But, my dear Meredith, make very sure you know whose fear is stopping you. Yours or his. Make very sure.''

Meredith reached over and clasped the old woman's hand.

''Thank you, Annabelle. For everything.''

''Then I have convinced you to come to tea—often?''

''Absolutely.''

The slender, papery fingers gave Meredith's hand an answering squeeze. ''Good. Tell me what I should do with that funny, lopsided lamp. Do you think I might be allowed to keep it? My grandfather was so proud of it.''

''Then you'll keep it, of course. But you could put it on a new table, if you like.'' Meredith didn't want to think of anything else except how to bring some light into this house. She didn't want to think about Annabelle's words, yet they haunted her even as she chatted of lampshades and curtain fringes. *''Make sure you know whose fear is stopping you. . . . Make very sure.''*

As she left Annabelle's house, Meredith forced herself to acknowledge her own fear. On her last day with Cal, she was the one to run away. She hadn't been brave enough to stay and take a risk with him. Yes, the risk was monumental; perhaps Cal would never love her. But she had to give him a chance. She had to be with him, doing everything she could to convince him that he did love her.

Meredith's heart lightened. She was suddenly filled with hope, and she spent the rest of the afternoon foraging through old bookshops, until she found what she was looking for.

Very early the next morning she drove back to the House of the Seasons, a package beside her. Heart thumping, she pulled into the drive. This was taking all her courage—more than she really possessed. Yet she knew Annabelle was right. She had to face her fears. She had to take a chance. All her happiness depended on it.

The Jaguar wasn't there. A lot of TLC and the new coat of white paint made the house look itself again. And a FOR SALE sign was pounded ruthlessly into the grass that was beginning to thrive again.

''No. No! You can't do this, Cal Bonner!'' But he was not there to hear her.

* * *

Meredith walked restlessly back and forth in the office of Quentin Fortsen, real estate agent. What was keeping the man? She was ready to fight out terms with him. She'd need to fight, because she didn't have a down payment for the house. But she was determined to own the House of the Seasons. No one could stop her—least of all Cal.

According to Ellen's information, Cal was still out of town and couldn't be reached. More than likely he didn't want to be reached. So be it. There was nothing she could do about that. He had, however, abandoned the house, and it was up to her to rescue it.

"Come on, Mr. Fortsen," she said impatiently. She spoke in a loud, belligerent voice. The door burst open, and Meredith found herself looking straight into Cal's blue-green eyes. She held on to the back of a chair, willing her heart to calm its absurd pounding. With an effort, she tilted her chin. "Hello, Cal," she said coolly.

"So you're the prospective buyer," he answered, his voice rough. "I'm sorry, Meredith, but I've decided not to sell the house."

Anger blazed through her. "Surely you can see it belongs with me," she declared. "I'm the one who loves it!"

"I'm the one who bought it in the first place. Don't you think I care about it?"

They glared at each other across Mr. Fortsen's desk.

"Frankly, no. I don't think you care in the least."

Mr. Fortsen hovered around them, buttoning and unbuttoning his gold blazer. "I'm sure we can come to a suitable arrangement," he murmured placatingly.

"The house is mine," Meredith said.

"I'm not selling," Cal returned.

"You don't have any choice. I'll—I'll sue if I have to."

"On what grounds?"

"I'll think of something."

"I don't know what to say," Mr. Fortsen said.

"I do," Meredith muttered, striding out of the office. "This isn't over yet, Cal Bonner!"

Next morning a loud knock rousted Meredith from sleep. She awoke in the cool dawn light, struggled into her robe, and padded down the stairs. Could it be Cal? Please. . . .

She yanked the door open, only to find a young man in a khaki uniform with a patch over the shirt pocket that indentified him as "Mike," a messenger from something called Express Delivery.

"Are you Meredith Grant?" he asked.

She nodded, and he shoved an envelope into her hand, then headed back to the motorcycle parked at the curb. Meredith tore open the envelope and scanned the single sheet inside. The handwriting was bold, decisive:

You are hereby ordered to appear posthaste at the House of the Seasons.

She leaned against the door, clutching the sheet in one hand and wiping away her tears with the other. Then she smiled. Cal thought he could commandeer her again, and this time he was right. She hurried back up the stairs and slipped into jeans and her favorite flowered shirt. She brushed out her hair and tried to dab on some mascara and lipstick. The job was thorougly botched and she had to start all over again. At last she was ready, and ran out to her van.

When she got to Cal's house, she found him waiting by the library mantel. He regarded her solemnly.

"Hello," he said.

"Hi."

"Do you think we can be together without drawing blood?"

"We can try." She felt tears gather in her eyes and spill over the bottom of her lashes onto her cheeks. She looked away from Cal.

He saw, though. "Meredith, you can't cry. Not now. I have something for you."

She was forced to look at him again. He held out a small bouquet of violets.

"Oh, Cal . . ." The flowers were crushed between their bodies.

"Tell me what I have to do," he pleaded huskily against her ear. "Because I'll do anything. I can't live apart from you. That's all there is to it, Meredith."

She pressed her face against his chest. "Just be here with me."

"I love you, Red."

She looked up at him, joy rising like a geyser in her throat. "I love you, too, rich boy."

It was a long while before he lifted his mouth from hers. "My Red," he murmured, stroking her hair. "If only you knew . . . okay, I'll admit it. You scared the wits out of me that day you said you loved me. I'd done such a good job convincing myself I was meant to be a bachelor . . . I was even a *happy* bachelor . . . and then you burst into my life, with all your colors and flowers."

She pressed herself closer to him. "I'm here to stay," she said.

He kissed one eyebrow, then the tip of her nose. "You'd better be." He held her tightly. "I think I've loved you since that first day. There you were, trying to hide your delectable body in that business suit.''

"It took me a little longer to fall for you," she said, mock-seriously. ''It wasn't until I saw you in a bath towel.''

He chuckled, then ravished her mouth again. She clung to him, feeling decidedly unsteady. Cal traced the line of her widow's peak with his finger.

"I kept trying to fight my love for you, Meredith. You were shaking up my entire life, and I resisted as long and as hard as I could. I flew to France last week. I thought if I got away from here I'd be able to see things more clearly. I saw them, all right. I saw what a fool I'd been—afraid to admit I loved you. I guess all along I'd known that you were the only woman who could change my life—deep down, where it really mattered. That was pretty scary.''

"I was afraid, too, Cal. I thought loving you meant losing all my freedom. Now I know I can't be free without you.''

"You'll never lose your independence with me, Red. All I want is to share my life with you. Here, in Crystal Creek. I'm buying the *Chronicle* from Sunmedia.''

Meredith drew back so she could look at him. "Cal, that's wonderful! I'm so happy for you. I'm so happy for both of us! But I almost forgot. I have a present for you, too.''

The book was bound in old leather, its gold tooling chipped and faded. Cal turned the yellowed pages carefully. *"You Can't Go Home Again."* He grinned. "My favorite. How did you know?''

She shrugged mischievously. ''I read minds.''

"I'm very glad I'm going to marry you, Red. Will you marry me?''

''If you insist.''

He kissed her again, tenderly. ''This old house needs us. We can't let it down, can we?''

''No, we can't,'' she answered softly. His arms enfolded her. She nestled blissfully against his shoulder. There were no barriers to keep her from him now. She was home at last.